INVASION FROM A WANDERING WORLD

The coming of the planet Xenephrene to the solar system had caused complete chaos on Earth, as the world's axis was shifted by the powerful new gravitational effects from the strange planet. The entire Northern Hemisphere became uninhabitable, and Earth's population and governments were forced to evacuate hurriedly to South America, Africa and Australia. Panic and riots broke out, and the world's overburdened governments were powerless to control them.

That was the situation when the first spaceship from Xenephrene landed on Earth and threw up a red barrage so deadly that Earth's most powerful weapons were annihilated on contact.

Then came a second visitor from the mysterious planet: a beautiful young girl with silver hair and innocent dark eyes, who brought a warning and àn appeal from the people of her world.

A BRAND NEW WORLD

Ray Cummings

WILDSIDE PRESS

To
Elizabeth Starr Hill
dearly loved daughter

I

THE COMING OF THE WORLD

THE NEW PLANET was first observed on the night of October 4, 1966, reported by the Clarkson Observatory, near London. A few hours later the observers at Washington saw it also; and still later, it was found and identified as unknown upon one of the photographic plates of the great refracting telescope at Flagstaff, Arizona. It was not seen by observers at Table Mountain, Cape Town, and the observatory near Buenos Aires, for it was in the northern heavens.

The affair brought a brief mention in the Amalgamated Broadcasters' report the next day; and the newspapers carried a few lines of it on their back pages. Nothing more.

I handled the item. My name is Peter Vanderstuyft. I was twenty-three years old, that autumn of 1966, a newsgatherer for the Amalgamated Broadcasters, attached to the New York City headquarters. The item meant nothing to me. It was the forerunner—the significant, tiny beginning—of the most terrible period of the history of the Earth; but I did not know that. I tossed it over to Freddie Smith, who was with me in the office that night.

"Father's staff has found a new star—wonderful!"

But Freddie's freckled face did not answer my grin. For once his pale blue eyes were solemn. "Professor Vanderstuyft phoned me from Washington awhile ago. It sure seems queer."

"What's queer?" I demanded.

Then he grinned. "Nope. Your father says you'd sell your soul for a news item. When we've got anything important to tell the world—we'll tell you."

"Go wrap up an electric spark," I informed him.

He grinned again and went back to studying his interminable blueprints—his "thermodyne principle," as he called it, for a new heatray motor. Father was financing him for the patents and working model. Freddie was father's assistant in the Washington Observatory. But he was off duty now in New York arranging for the manufacture of his model.

This was in October. I was tremendously busy. A sensational murder case developed, and I was sent out to Indiana to cover it. A woman had presumably murdered her husband and a couple of children, but it looked as though she were going to be acquitted.

She was a handsome woman, and a good talker. She was taking full advantage of the new law regarding free speech, and every night from the jail she was broadcasting little talks to the public.

October passed, and then November, and still I had not been able to get back to New York. Freddie occupied my rooms there, busy with his invention; father was at his post in Washington, and my sister Hulda was in Puerto Rico, visiting our friends the Cains. Our plans—father's and mine—were to join the Cains and Hulda in Puerto Rico for Christmas.

Father was leaving the Washington Observatory to assume charge of the Royal Dutch Astronomical Bureau, which had just completed an observatory in extreme Southern Chile, with the largest telescope in the world soon to be installed there. Freddie Smith was going with him as his assistant;

and the A.B. Association had appointed me their representative, to live down there also.

None of these plans worked out, however. Christmas approached, and I was still engaged in Indiana with this accursed broadcasting murderess. And father wired me that he was too busy in Washington to leave.

During all these weeks there had been continual items in the news concerning the new planet—issued by father's Washington staff, and by most of the observatories in the northern hemisphere. Father is a queer character; the Holland blood in us makes us phlegmatic, silent, and cautious—characteristics which apply more to father than to me. He is a true scientist, calmly judicial, unwilling to judge anything or form any decisive opinion without every possible fact before him.

Thus it was that during those weeks neither Hulda in Puerto Rico nor I had an intimation from father of the startling things he was learning. As he said finally, of what use to worry us until he was sure? Like the public in general, I became aware of conditions gradually. A news item here and there—items growing more insistent as the weeks passed, but still all crowded aside to make room for the sensational murder trial.

I recall some of the items. The new planet was approaching the general region of our solar system with extraordinary velocity. A planet of the fortieth magnitude. Then they said it was the thirtieth. Soon it was visible to the naked eye. I remember reading one account, not long after the planet's discovery, in which its spectrum was reported to be sunlight! Our own solar spectrum! Reflected sunlight! This was no distant, gigantic, incandescent star blazing with its own light. It was not large and far away, but small and close. As small as our own Earth, and already it was within the limits of our solar system. A dark globe, like our Earth, or the moon, or Venus and Mars—dark and solid, shining only by reflected sunlight!

By mid-December, at a convention of astronomers held in London, the new world was named Xenephrene. Father went over in one of the mail planes and read his afterward

7

famous paper, suggesting the name, and giving his calculation of the elements of the orbit of this new heavenly body. It was the most startling announcement which had yet been made, and for one newspaper edition it got the first page. And I was ordered to give nine minutes of broadcasting time to it.

"Xenephrene" was a globe not quite, but very nearly, as large as the Earth. It had come whirling in like a comet from the star-filled regions of outer space; presumably like a comet to encircle our sun and then, with a hyperbolic orbit, to depart from us forever.

It had come visually into our northern heavens, and crossed the Earth's orbit on the opposite side of the sun from us. It circled the sun—this was in December—made its turn between the orbits of Mercury and Venus, and now was supposedly departing.

But according to father's calculation of its new orbital elements, it was not about to depart! Its orbit had become an ellipse—a very nearly circular ellipse similar to those of Venus and the Earth! A new planet—a brand new world—had joined our solar family! A world only a fraction smaller than Venus and the Earth; larger than Mars, larger than Mercury. An interior planet, its orbit would be within that of the Earth—between the Earth and Venus.

On this date, December 20—so ran father's announcement—Xenephrene was proceeding in its elliptical orbit, and the Earth was in advance of it. We could see Xenephrene in the sky now—anyone could see it who cared to look. It was no more than thirty million miles from us now. A new morning and evening star, which at times far outshone Venus.

See it indeed! Xenephrene, the magnificent! For weeks it had been visible throughout its erratic course as from the great unknown realms of outer space it swam into our ken. During October and November it had been visually too near the sun—and too far away as yet—to be much of a spectacle. But I saw it in early December, just before dawn, a morning star rising in the eastern· sky. A glowing

8

purple spot of light, blazing like a great sapphire in the pale gray-blue of the dawn.

Xenephrene, the new world! I stood gazing up at it, and a flood of romance surged over me. A new world, strange, mysterious, beautiful! I had occasion several times during those terrible, fearsome days which so soon were to come to all of us on Earth, to recall my fleeting mood of romance at first sight of Xenephrene. Mysterious globe! Romantic! How well could I have added—sinister!

What the scientists were thinking and doing during these weeks of December, 1966, and January, 1967, I did not know until later. Their fears, gropings, unceasing labor to verify their dawning suspicion of the truth, they withheld from the public. Until father's culminating discovery, which he made public on February 10, 1967.

Christmas that winter was a depressing time for all of us. I think, everywhere in the world, a sense of ominous depression was gradually spreading. A great catastrophe impending, even though unheralded, must inevitably cast its forerunning shadow. I know I felt depressed, away from father and Hulda, alone out there in Indiana on my job, with father inexplicably too busy to let me join him.

Hulda's Christmas letter from Puerto Rico was depressing: Miserable winter. Peter, it's positively cold. Imagine—we had it 54 degrees yesterday. In Puerto Rico! Mrs. Cain says we wish you'd keep your icy blasts of the north to yourself. She was trying to be jocular, but Hulda too was depressed that Christmas. It was indeed a miserable winter. Extraordinarily cold, everywhere. For a week or two, the papers had been commenting upon it. Zero weather around New York and all out through Indiana to Chicago. A succession of gray, snowy days—gray afternoons with the twilight seeming to come in mid-afternoon. And at nearly eight o'clock in the morning it was still the twilight of dawn. The newspapers commented on that, jocularly remarking that the weather man was making our winter days short this year.

The weather, in truth, was so abnormal that it occasioned an increasing newspaper comment. Even by Christmas, Canada was enveloped by constant sub-zero temperatures, which occasionally swept down as far as Virginia with heavy snowfalls. Florida, in December, had its greatest freeze since 1888; damage to the fruit was enormous. In the West Indies, an unprecedented cool wave was experienced.

Everywhere in the north temperate zone it was the same. And from South America we had the reverse reports. The summer in Rio and in Buenos Aires was unusually hot. Cape Town reported an abnormal spell; Australia and New Zealand were sweltering.

And there were other strange effects. Our winter days, for instance, were abnormally short. It was not fancy; it seemed an actual fact. And from the southern hemisphere reports gave reverse conditions. The days were growing unnaturally long; sunset and twilight extended abnormally far into the evening.

It occurred to me as strange that our A.B.A. never broadcasted a mention of this; that there were never any scientific, authoritative reports concerning it. Surely the scientists could determine with exactitude whether our sun were rising and setting at the times it should! They could, indeed! They could—and they were calculating it only too exactly! But, as I learned afterward, there was a world government censorship upon the whole subject.

This censorship was lifted on that memorable February 10, 1967, when father made his startling statement to the world.

On February 9th, my job in Indiana ended; the murderess was acquitted amid applause and public rejoicing. But the verdict only held a divided first-page place now with the planet Xenephrene. The new world had steadily been nearing the Earth; it was now only twenty-odd million miles away—a magnificent spectacle, a purple point of light blazing near the sun; with the naked eye it appeared twice the size of any star.

In the afternoon of February 9th, Freddie phoned me from New York. I had never heard his voice so strangely solemn.

"Pete, your father wants you to come to Washington at once."

10

"What's up?" I demanded.

"Nothing. He wants to see you and me. You come to New York—join me here—leave today. Will you?"

"Yes," I agreed. "I'm through out here, fortunately."

"I'll wait for you here at your place. I wouldn't try the planes, if I were you—not with storms like this. Come by train; it's safer."

He was so solemn! It wasn't like Freddie Smith to bother about safety—a daredevil, if there ever was one. But he was right about the planes; the surest way to get to New York at the moment was to take it slowly.

For a week the whole western United States had been locked in the grip of a blizzard. The railroads were hung up; the strain of traffic and the fearful weather had been too much for the passenger planes. Every one was jammed; and several failed to get through and were stalled in the storm along the way. But the railroads now were getting their tracks cleared; service was improving.

"I'll see you tomorrow," I told Freddie.

"Yes," he said. "I've got our accommodations on board the Congressional. Get here if you can."

I got through, and we took the Congressional Limited for Washington. New York City was an almost unprecedented sight that dark-gray afternoon we left. It might have been a snowbound Canadian city, by its appearance. A heavy, silent fall of snow, thick, soft, pure-white flakes.

The north wind of the past few days had died away. The snow sifted almost vertically down between the canyons of buildings. Without a wind, the afternoon seemed only moderately cold. Freddie and I passed a street thermometer at the corner where we had gone to join our taxi, which could not get into the cross-street. The temperature was five below zero.

Freddie caught my expression. He said, "This isn't New York cold. Can't you tell the difference? This is the cold of the north."

Our taxi with its clanking chains rumbled its way down Broadway and across to the Station. A white sheet, piled with soft, white snow which covered up its familiar con-

11

figurations, buried its curbs, leveled street and pedestrian walks into one flat white surface. A strange Broadway: featureless, blankly expressionless, like a man's face without hair or eyebrows.

There was little traffic. Pedestrians in a crowd tramped the street's center. In the still cold the snow creaked and crunched under their tread.

At the shop windows, almost closed in by huge piles of snow left over from the storm of the week before, disconsolate proprietors gazed out from under the shadow of the overhead pedestrian levels. Three o'clock in the afternoon; the street lights were all winking on, turning the pure white of the snow a pale lurid green with their glare.

The crowd seemed taking it like a holiday, gay with shouts of laughter as people romped and shoved their way through the drifts. But there was no laughter within me. "The cold of the north," Freddie had said. It brought me a vague shudder.

"Look there." Freddie pointed to the second level at Forty-Second Street. At a department store entrance crowds were coming out and going in. A huge sign in moving electric lights gave the information that here Canadian winter equipment could be purchased. And as I gazed, a man in gaudy flannel costume of brilliant colors came from the store entrance. An advertisement, no doubt. He swung out to the pedestrian level on skis, poised, and came sliding gracefully down the incline to the main street level, amid shouts and applause from the crowd.

We humans adjust ourselves very quickly to new conditions. And, for all the pessimists to the contrary, the human instinct is to laugh. . . . I saw a canvas sign over a small store, on a cross-street impassable at the moment with snowdrifts. It bore the ancient quip, "Whether the weather be cold or hot, we've got to have weather, whether or not. Buy your Arctic overshoes here."

New York City, that February 10th, thought it was all a good joke. . . .

Freddie and I had a compartment on the Congressional.

We anticipated it would be nearly midnight by the time we got to Washington; Freddie flung himself moodily on the lounge as though he were prepeared to sleep all the way, except when we might perhaps order in dinner.

Freddie at this time was twenty-seven. I had always liked him, though physically and temperamentally we were quite opposite types. I am typically Dutch, short and wide, heavy-set and stocky. But not fat. Built, as Freddie once told me, along the general lines of a young cart horse. And, as he has also remarked, I have the Dutch phlegmatic sparseness of speech, which in my case, he insists, often turns surly.

Freddie, not much taller than I, was slender almost to thinness. But wiry; I have wrestled with him, and he twists like an eel, with surprising strength. A sandy-haired, pale-blue-eyed, freckled-faced fellow, usually grinning, and with a swift, ready flow of speech.

His mind not only was alert, but keen. Scientifically in-clined; and an extremely good mathematician. He had made good at astronomical work from the start. As a clocker of delicate star-transits, in father's opinion he had no equal; and he could sit all day over tedious routine mathematics and never tire.

I eyed him now as he lay on the lounge in our train compartment. It was wholly abnormal for Freddie to be so morose.

"Whatever it is father's got to tell me," I commented, "it sits like lead on you, doesn't it?"

"Yes," he said abruptly. And he added, "He ordered me to say nothing, so I'm doing it."

I found father equally solemn. It was eleven o'clock when after crossing the snow-filled Washington streets we reached my home. Father greeted us at the door with what was a very sick attempt at a smile.

"Come in, boys. You're lucky to get here at all. Hello, Frederick. Brought your model? That's good—we'll look at it presently. . . . Hello, son—I understand you've been pampering a murderess."

In the study, when we had discarded our overclothes, his manner abruptly changed. We sat down, and he stood facing us, and then began restlessly pacing the little circular room, as though undecided how to begin telling me.

"Peter," he said at last, "you'll think it's queer that I've said nothing to you, my son, of this—this thing that is upon us now—this catastrophe to the world—"

My heart leaped. Yet it was hardly a surprise. Knowledge of it all had been coming to me little by little for weeks; fragments here and there, like the meaningless parts of a puzzle which now his words, adding nothing new, pieced together to make my premonitions a complete realization. He spoke swiftly, fronting me with his squared, heavy shoulders; his dark eyes holding me with his somber gaze.

"No use to worry you, son, or to frighten Hulda—you could be of no help—and we're all in it together, the whole world. . . .They've lifted the censorship. The time has come when it is best for everyone to know it—this inevitable thing. Peter, you can give it to your organization tonight, and to the world. The widest publicity—this statement from me and my organization—"

He stopped abruptly, seeming to realize the incoherence of his words, striving to master his emotions and tell me calmly. He seized a chair and sat facing me, smiling at Freddie; and he lighted a cigar.

But his fingers trembled. He was a man of sixty at this time; a squarely solid, commanding figure; a smooth-shaven face, square-jawed, dark, restless eyes, with gray-black, bushy brows and a shock of iron-gray hair. A crisp, forceful speaker. But he had not been so tonight. I have never seen him look so old, almost haggard. And the usual clear white of his eyes was shot with blood.

I understood it as he talked; past weeks of anxiety, nights of sleepless observation at the telescope, watching Xenephrene, the new world; watching it come in to join our little solar family; observing by night—and all day busy with unending calculations of Xenephrene's changing orbit as it rounded the sun and took its place among us.

Watching—at first with interest, surprise, awe; then with a dawning fear. Then, his hurried conferences with other scientists. He had been three times to London, I now learned—and once, a consultation of astronomers was held at the Chan observatory, in Tibet.

And then, conferences of the scientists with the world governments, at which time the censorship was ordered. And father went back to his post, to observe and calculate the daily abnormal changes in our sunrise and sunset. Until at last the truth could no longer be escaped. The future could be prognosticated, to a mathematical certainty; the censorship must be lifted and the world told.

Father's voice, with its old dominating ring now, boomed at me.

"The world must be told, Peter. We cannot, dare not, hide it any longer. This new planet Xenephrene—I'll give you all the technical details; I have them here." He waved a sheaf of typewritten papers at me. "Your office can prepare it in any form you like. The coming of Xenephrene—its new bulk so near us—had disturbed, is now disturbing, our Earth. You know it—everybody knows it instinctively, through they don't realize it or understand it."

"The weather—" I began; and my pounding heart seemed nearly smothering me.

"Yes—the weather. And our queerly shortened winter days. All these abnormal conditions which have come upon us this winter. Xenephrene has affected us astronomically in just one way. The inclination of the axis of our Earth is altering. Do you know what that really means? Can you explain it to the public?"

"He can," Freddie burst out. "He will."

The axis of the Earth! Our seasons—our winter and summer—our climate—our days and nights—changing, permanently changing? It seemed, for an instant, nothing. And then it seemed a thought too amazing, too unnatural to encompass. The basic order of everything from time immemorial now to be changed? And as I listened to his swift, brusque words my head reeled.

The axis of the Earth was slowly swinging so that eventually our South Pole would point directly to the sun and there became stabilized. This would occur by next April 5.

15

Our new seasons, our new astronomical year, would begin on that date.

"Can you realize what that will mean, Peter? When our South Pole points to the sun there will be a torrid zone in the southern hemisphere. The great antarctic polar continent will blaze into a tropical glory. Patagonia, the Magellan Straits, Australia, the Federated Cape Provinces, far southern Chile and the Argentine—all in the blazing tropics. Six months of that, with days months long in which the sun never sets! Then swinging back to winter.

"The new temperate zone will be at our equator. Not very temperate. Snow and ice alternating with months of blazing heat. And all our northern hemisphere—it will have six months, beginning next April, of total darkness and frightful cold."

His voice rose to a grim power. "Ah, you're beginning to realize what it will mean to us! New seasons, and new periods of day and night! Blazing noon at the South Pole! Dark, silent, congealed midnight in the north. Darkness like a cold black shroud over most of our northern hemisphere. Our greatest cities are here, Peter. London, New York, Paris, Berlin, Tokyo, Peking—from forty to fifty North Latitude. All will be buried for months in the darkness of arctic night!"

He laughed just a little wildly. "Some people think it is a joke now, this strange new winter which has descended upon us. In New York they're beginning to treat it like a Canadian winter carnival. Fun while it lasts, and then spring and summer will come soon again—because they always have before. But this time, Peter, spring and summer won't come soon again.

"The winter will grow colder. They have only seen its carnival aspect so far. But the cold of the north has fangs. It's a monster—a hideous monster whose congealing breath is death. It's lurking up there, ready to creep upon us. It's in Canada now, in north Asia, in northern Europe.

"They're laughing in New York because it gets dark so early in the afternoon. It's fun to tumble in the snow in the early afternoon twilight. But they won't laugh in another

16

week or two. The blessed sunlight for New York is almost gone. Shorter days—still shorter—until soon there will be no day at all!

"Our huge cities here in the north, all buried in the snow and ice and darkness of a polar winter! The greatest catastrophe in the history of the world—we're facing it now! No power on Earth can help us to escape it, for it's inevitable!"

II

THE WHITE GIRL IN THE MOONLIGHT

THE PLANTATIONS of the Cains in Puerto Rico lay back from the north coast, some thirty kilometers from San Juan. Bisected by the railroad and by the main auto road, they spread green and fragrant in the vivid sunlight. Rows of orange and grapefruit trees, stretching over the undulating sand, with pineapples between the rows of trees.

Here and there, thickets of banana trees, encouraged to grow and break the force of the trade wind from the sea; a tall spreading mango—a sapling perhaps back in the almost forgotten days when Spain ruled this island; occasional clumps of giant coconuts rising on the low hillsides; trees with smooth brown trunks and feather-duster tops, the trunks all bent backward from the coast by the wind.

The main auto road, lined with its majestic royal palms, was oily black and sometimes very noisy; the railroad with its metal ties was a dark streak like a double pencil line amid the green of the trees. But the plantation crossroads were white ribbons of sand in the sunlight, and whiter still at night, under the white glory of the moon.

It was then, at night, that the magic romance of the tropics was to me always most poignant. At sundown the brisk trades were stilled. A quiet, brooding somnolence fell upon everything. The native shacks, palm-thatched, burned brown by the sun, turned darkly mysterious. Off beyond

17

the distant coast, as it showed from the commanding height of the Cains' veranda, the sea at night was dimly purple under a gem-studded purple sky; and sometimes the moonbeams shimmered off there in the silent magic darkness. The scent of the orange blossoms hung heavy in the still air, exotic, stirring the fancy to a million half formed dreams that one may tell but never express.

Upon the highest knoll, an eminence of perhaps a hundred feet, stood the Cains' plantation house. A white road led up the slope to it. A broad, spreading frame bungalow, with a peaked tin roof, and a wide flat veranda around three of its sides, with coconut posts set at intervals. A bunch of bananas always hung there, ripening; a box lying against the house wall was filled with oranges at intervals by a native boy.

Beyond the house, at the edge of the knoll-top, a corral with open sides and heavy thatched roof housed the saddle and workhorses. The Cains' one concession to modernity—the garage, and a small hangar for Dan's sport plane—stood well beyond the foot of the knoll. In the evening, lolling in the wicker chairs on the veranda, one could not see the garage, and if the traffic on the main road chanced to be dull, one might go back in fancy half a century, to when this magic land must have been at its best. It was still very beautiful. Sunlight and color and warmth.

But the blight, here as everywhere else in the northern hemisphere, was already at hand.

"Tomorrow," said Dan, "we'll ride over to Arecibo. Want to, Hulda?"

"On horseback?"

"Yes," he said. "You don't think, knowing you as I do, I'd insult you with a car or a plane?"

Hulda can drive a car or handle a plane as well as any one. But for all our Dutch stolidity, there is a strain of romance in us. Hulda's greatest pleasure was riding astride the little Puerto Rican horses; and though there seems nothing hotter on Earth than a white sand road at noon in the cane fields, Hulda would always ride through them with delight.

18

"Good," she said, and laughed, "Señor Dan, that will please me much."

But her mocking laugh was forced, for this was February 10th of that fateful winter. An unknown fear lay upon Hulda, as on us all; and the cane fields on the way to Arecibo might have been hot other years, but they certainly were not hot now.

This evening, for instance, as Mr. and Mrs. Cain and their son Dan, and Hulda, sat in the living room of the bungalow, the shutters were all closed and a huge brazier of charcoal burned beside them for warmth. Already it had smoked up the ceiling; and Mr. Cain, despairing that the cool spell would soon moderate, promised his wife for the tenth time that he would get a stove from San Juan and rig it up all shipshape with a pipe—"Like in Vermont, eh, Ellen? Hulda, I'm going to radio your father tomorrow. This local weather bureau's too dumb to tell me anything. Your father ought to know—he's a scientist; they're supposed to know everything."

The Cains were what, a decade or so ago, were called plain folks. New Englanders, Cain had made his money on a Vermont farm. Their only son Dan had grown to manhood and graduated from college with one of the new agricultural degrees; and partly because of Mrs. Cain's frail health they had taken Dan and established themselves in Puerto Rico.

Dan now was the brains and the energy of the business. I had gone to school with Dan Cain. A big, rangy, husky, six-footer, with crisp, curly brown hair, blue eyes and a laughing boyish sun-tanned face.

A handsome young giant, I should imagine any girl would love him at sight. Demure little Hulda, a brown sparrow of a girl, loved him, I felt certain, though nothing as yet had been said of any engagement between them. I rather hoped it would come to pass; and I think Dan's parents did also, for Hulda was very lovable.

Life often holds odd coincidences. At eleven o'clock, this night of February 10, I was in Washington with father and Freddie. What father was telling me I thought then the most important event of the world's welfare.

But at almost the same time, Hulda, in Puerto Rico, was sitting in the living room with Dan Cain. And another event, wholly different in significance yet of equal importance to the world, was impending. The elder Cains had retired. Dan and Hulda, characteristic of them of late when alone, had fallen into sober discussion.

Dan was really perturbed over the weather. The temperature had gone far into the forties the night before. It certainly was not good for Puerto Rican trees. And the Florida citrus industry was wiped out this winter. It had snowed last week all over the peninsula; a fall of snow with a following freeze that had killed everything which the December freeze had spared. And now—into the forties in Puerto Rico! Ten degrees lower would be freezing. If this went on—

The sound of a pony thudding up the knoll at a gallop broke in upon Hulda's and Dan's gloomy reflections. They stared at each other.

"What could that be?" Dan was on his feet.

The pony came up to the front porch entrance, stopped, and on the wooden steps bare feet sounded. Dan flung open the door. The pale-blue vacuum light newly established in the Puerto Rican rural districts was behind him; the doorway was a dark rectangle of brilliant stars and cold moonlight, and a rush of chill air swept in.

A peon was on the porch, dirty white trousers and white shirt, ghostly in the moonlight. He was barefooted and bareheaded. His little white pony stood at the foot of the steps in a lather of sweat, drooping and panting.

"Ramon!" Dan exclaimed. "What the devil! Come in here!"

It was one of the Cain's house boys. He came in, chattering, but not from cold. His coffee-colored face had a green cast with its pallor. He was frightened almost beyond speech.

"What the devil!"

Dan shook the boy with annoyance. Hulda stood apart, staring, and a nameless fear was on her; an unreasonable shudder as though this thing—in its outward aspect the mere

20

fright of a native boy, which probably meant nothing important—were something gruesome, horrible, unutterably frightening.

"Ramon—"Dan shook him again, and the boy suddenly poured out a flood of Spanish, broken, incoherent. Hulda could not understand it. She saw Dan's face grow grave, and then he laughed. But it struck Hulda then that the incredulous laugh had a note of fear in it.

"Ramon, que dice?" The boy understood English. Dan added, "Don't be a fool, Ramon! Tell me—"

Hulda asked anxiously, "What is it, Dan?"

He swung on her, and as he saw her face, the solemn fear in her dark eyes, his laugh faded.

"Hulda, he says he was riding home from a fiesta over at the Rolf plantation in Factor. Coming back—you know the hills back there where the bat caves are—what we call our Eden tract? He saw something—a woman like a ghost, he says. A woman's figure that jumped—it's out there now."

Ramon had shrunk against the wall, shuddering; the whites of his black eyes glistened in the blue glare of the vacuum tube.

"Ramon, you been drinking?"

"No! Oh, no—no, señor!"

"What else, Dan?"

Hulda wanted to laugh. It was funny, paying serious attention to a native's devil story. Other years, an Americano señor would laugh at any peon who talked of a ghost he had seen in the moonlight. But not now; there was an uncanniness in the very air everywhere in the world this winter.

The boy was quieter. He told Dan more and Dan soberly translated it. A thing like a great round silver ball, big as a native shack, glistening with the moonlight on it as it lay in a coconut grove, a mile from the Cains' plantation house, near the hills where the bat caves are.

Ramon's pony had suddenly shied, and then Ramon had seen the gleaming white thing lying there. And then he had seen a figure like that of a woman or a girl—a white girl, with flowing white hair.

21

It was quite near him, standing beside the sloping trunk of a big palm tree that grew on the hillside. Twenty foot away, perhaps, and ten feet higher than the trail along which he was riding.

Ramon was stiff with fear. His pony halted; it stood with upraised head and pointing ears. It saw the white woman's motionless figure and suddenly raised its head with a long shuddering neigh of fear. The sound must have startled the white woman up there. Ramon saw her crouch; then she leaped from the hillside.

His pony bolted. And then he lashed it for home, fearing the thing was chasing him.

Dan was very solemn. "That doesn't sound like a ghost tale, Hulda. Ramon, saddle our ponies. Mine—Parti-blanco —and the señorita's. Not with the aparejo—with the man's saddle."

He glanced at Hulda, her trim figure in leather puttees and brown riding trousers. Her face was now almost as white as her blouse.

She stammered, "You want to go out there—go and see—"

Ramon whimpered, "Señor, I'm afraid, here at the corral —if it followed after me!"

Dan strode to the porch. The broad spread of the plantations lay solemn and still under the cold white moon. The thatched roof of the corral was dark, with inky black shadows beside the building. The banana trees arching up over the house waved gently in the night breeze. Everything was sharply white and black. But there was no sign of any intruder, human or otherwise.

"I'll go with you to saddle the ponies, Ramon. We'll go—you want to go Hulda?"

"Yes," she said. She felt at that moment too frightened to stay in the house without Dan, and thought of the elder Cains asleep in the adjoining room never occurred to either of them.

With sweaters donned against the midnight cold, they saddled the ponies and started.

Dan rode ahead, with Hulda almost beside him, and Ramon, his pony as reluctant as himself, following after them. It was a brief ride during which they hardly spoke. Down the knoll, past the silent garage; past the somnolent group of shacks of the plantation workers.

The road was narrow—white sand like a trail. Coconut trees arched it in places, and beside it spread the tracts of fruit trees. It wound back toward a low-lying range of hills and up a steep declivity, where it turned stony from the rain water which daily washed down it.

Dan was flinging watchful glances around them. "Don't see anything yet, Hulda. Do you?" His voice was a cautious half whisper.

The sure-footed ponies picked their way carefully up the stony trail. They went through a little ravine and emerged into a small valley, a plateau almost flat on this higher land. Hills a hundred feet high fenced it in; its table-like surface of white sand was ruled off with the dark green lines of fruit trees. It was the Cains' two-hundred acre "Eden tract". It lay brooding and drowsy under the moon, without a sign of human movement.

Dan halted; Ramon's pony came beside him.

"Where were you when you saw it, Ramon?"

The boy gestured. He was trembling again. He held his pony forcibly from wheeling to run back. The other ponies seemed to sense the terror. They raised their heads; one whimpered, and they were all quivering. But Dan forced them slowly forward.

The trail skirted the hills to the left. Above it, halfway up a steep ascent, three black yawning mouths of the bat-caves showed. Hulda had often been in them with Dan; a guano deposit in them was used as fertilizer for the trees. Hulda saw them now, round and black with the moonlight on the rocks beside them, fifty feet above the valley.

Ramon suddenly chattered: "There! You see it? Ave Maria—"

Off at the edge of the fruit trees, in the shadows of a clump of coconut palms, a great round thing gleamed. A silver sphere, like a white ball some twenty feet high, lying there. It was several hundred feet away, but Hulda could see a black rift in it. A crack? A doorway!

It had a sort of quality about it—a ball, not bouncing actually, but appearing, indefinably, translucent, almost weightless. She knew then, though not with conscious reasoning, what all this was to mean. A silver sphere lying there, with a black rift in it like a doorway, and a small black patch in its side—like a window!

"Hulda! Look!" Dan's hand went to her arm with a grip that both hurt and steadied her. The three ponies were standing with braced feet in the sand. Dan's flung up its head to neigh; but his fist thumped its head and stilled it.

And then Hulda saw the figure, as the native boy had seen it half an hour before. It was standing now near the trail ahead of them, between two orange trees; and just as Hulda saw it, the thing moved over, and stopped in the moonlight on the white trail, as though to bar their passage. It was not far ahead of them. Hulda could see it plainly. A white figure; but it did not shimmer. Not ghostly—white only because of the moonlight on it. Uncanny, weird, yet not gruesome.

It was the figure of a girl; small, as small as Hulda. A slim, pink-white girl's body, with flowing draperies which in daylight might have been sky-blue. Long white hair flowing over pink shoulders.

Dan's grip on Hulda tightened; then he cast her off and his hand caught her bridle reins and held her pony firmly. Behind them Ramon and his pony were thudding away in a panic.

Dan breathed, "It—she sees us!"

The girl's arms went slowly up as though with a gesture. It did not seem menacing; a gesture of fear perhaps. Pale-white arms, of delicate human shape. They were bare, but as they slowly raised, the folds of the drapery clung to them.

Abruptly Dan called, "Hello, there—"

The figure did not move further. But the ponies were becoming unmanageable. Dan exclaimed hastily, "Dismount, Hulda!—you'll be thrown off! I can hold them."

Hulda and Dan dismounted. But Dan could not hold the ponies. They jerked away from him. He and Hulda were

24

left standing in the sand of the trail, gazing after the two terror-stricken animals as they galloped away toward home.

Dan remembered later that there came to him then a fleeting wonderment. Why were these ponies so afraid of this white figure of a girl in the moonlight? From this distance there seemed nothing abut the figure unduly to frighten an animal. The question was not answered until long afterward. But there were indeed things about this white shape which the ponies evidently saw and felt— things which were denied to Hulda's and Dan's human senses.

Hulda gasped, "Oh, they've gone!" She stood by Dan, clinging to him. The white figure in the road was gone also. But in a moment more they saw it again—near to them now, not more than thirty feet away. It was standing off the trail among the fruit trees.

Dan murmured, "It's human, Hilda. Nothing to be afraid of—see, it's only a girl. You call to her."

Hulda's quavering voice floated out, "We see you. Who are you? We're friends."

The figure moved again: backward, floating or walking soundlessly but swiftly, as though with sudden fear.

"Come on," said Dan. He started briskly forward along the trail, with Hulda close after him. But within a dozen steps, he stopped. And then to both Dan and Hulda came amazement, and the thrill of real fear.

The figure had been retreating. But the hill was close behind it. Suddenly it stopped, seemed to gather itself, to crouch, to spring. It left the ground and sailed up into the unobstructed moonlight above the orange trees. Sailing up in an arc it passed almost directly over their heads and landed soundlessly in the road behind them!

As it passed overhead, outlined against the stars, they saw it more plainly. It seemed a girl of human form, cast in a fashion which might well have been called beautiful. She poised, not as though flying, but sailing. Face toward the ground, white hair waving behind her, arms outstretched, with the folds of her drapery robe opened fan-shaped, flutter-ing like wings. There was a brief glimpse of her lower limbs,

25

human of mold with the robe wound by the wind close around them.

A thing of beauty, had it not been so uncanny. She floated in a sailing arc as though almost weightless; and with a flip, dropped to the ground upright upon her feet. A fairy's leap! Soundless, graceful! Romantic, yet uncanny. A figure of enchantment from the dream of a child.

Dan tried to laugh. Fear seemed incongruous. As he and Hulda turned, the figure stood again in the trail facing them. And they could see it was a slim young girl, strangely beautiful, fearful as a fawn at their approach; yet she lingered, seeming—Dan wondered if his fancy were playing him tricks—desirous of conquering her fear and meeting them.

"Hulda—nothing to be afraid of. Don't move; you'll frighten her!"

They stood motionless. The white girl in the moonlight down the road took a step forward. They did not move. She came a little further, paused. Then another step. She was not floating, but walking—they could see the outlines of her limbs moving beneath the drapery.

And now he could see her face. Queer, strange of feature, yet in what way they could not have said. And certainly beautiful, gentle, anxious, and afraid. Youthful, a mere girl; and with those flowing waves of snow-white hair framing her face and falling thick over her pink-white shoulders.

She stood, twenty feet away. Dan and Hulda were almost holding their breaths. Dan murmured, "Speak to her again. Softly—don't frighten her!"

Hulda said gently, "Can you understand me? We're friends."

The strange girl stood birdlike, trembling. Hulda repeated, "We're friends—won't hurt you. Shall we come nearer? Who are you?"

There was a moment of silence. And then the girl spoke. A soft whisper of a voice, ethereal as the fairy voice of a child's enchanted fancy; a wraith of sound, but it carried, and Hulda and Dan heard it plainly.

"Zetta! Zetta! Zetta!"

III

THE CROWNING TERROR

THERE WAS so much happening everywhere in the world
during those fateful weeks that followed February 10, 1966
—events so startling, amazing, so stupendous of import,
and of such diversity that I scarce know how to recount
them.

There was a reckless abandonment of defense installations—
a frenzied urge for self-preservation, each individual, each
family fighting frantically for its survival. The government,
in all its branches, was disintegrating. Department after
department was abandoned by its personnel. Everywhere,
those who should give the orders were scattered, no one
knew where.

Orders? To fulfill any orders would have been impossible.
And for what? Every government on the Earth was in the
process of abandoning its projects, its ramified defenses,
recognizing no enemy save that which the elements created.

The world was incoherent—everywhere a chaos of events
unprecedented, uncontrollable. And in the chaos which
swept Freddie and me away, the news from Dan Cain in
Puerto Rico, important though it was, at the time concerned
us little.

Father was in constant communication with the Cains;
and later, after father had gone to Miami when the Federal
capital was moved there in flight from Washington, he
went to Puerto Rico.

The announcement that our world was to have such different days and nights, and a climate so utterly changed,
struck the public with horror.

It is not my purpose to try to detail or to picture it: the
chaos everywhere; the paralyzation of industry throughout
the northern hemisphere which so far had been proceeding

by man's will against all the invading efforts of nature to wreck it; the panics that took place in all the northern cities; crowds of refugees struggling to get south; inadequate transportation; accidents; and a horrible crime-wave that swept unchecked over every one of the large population centers.

Human activities in our modern world are very widely diversified; more widely so—and yet more intermingled, more interdependent—than anyone realizes until there comes an upset from the normal.

There is in these modern times nothing that anyone does which does not almost immediately affect what someone else is doing. Had the change come slowly, spread over a hundred, or a thousand or a hundred thousand years as other great world changes have come and passed, conditions would have adjusted themselves. No one would even have noticed the change.

But this was happening in minutes where others had taken centuries. New York, London, Paris and all the cities of the north were doomed to six months of twilight and night and blighting cold. Snow now was upon land, millions of acres of land, where crops soon must grow if millions of people were to have food. Yet now we knew those millions of acres would be for months snow-buried.

Millions of homes soon would be without adequate heat or light, and the people without adequate clothing. Rivers upon which the great power plants depended were congealing into ice.

This for the north, with business, industry and nearly every human activity paralyzed by the sudden public horror. But in the south, from the Equator to the South Pole, lay the land of promise. Or at least the public thought so.

Life lay there—life and the promise of food and warmth and blessed sunlight. For in the far Antarctic south, with the new light and heat coming, millions upon millions of acres of land would be springing into a new fertility to replace what the north had lost. But this, too, was a fallacy; for after a few months, the pendulum would swing back; the far south would go into night and cold.

Many hundred million people, suddenly giving up all their accustomed work in the world's activities and trying to move to another region! A migration greater than the sum total of all others in the world's history. In a hundred years of systematic, careful planning and execution it might have been accomplished without disaster. But now it was a panic, a chaos, a flight. Distracted governments tried to cope with it, but they were impotent to bring even a semblance of order.

Our office of the Amalgamated Broadcasters was maintained in New York City until well along in February. With government affiliation, we broadcasted only what might be of help to the public: news of conditions, generally censored to allay too great a fear; advice as to what to do; information concerning transportation; and news from the south. In this work, Freddie now joined me. There were days—almost dark now except for a brief time before and after midday—when he and I were in our cold office, one or the other of us at the microphone throughout the twenty-four hours.

It was an office of incoherent men and disorganized service; without light, some of the time; with frozen and burst heating pipes and no one to repair them. We sat bundled in our overcoats, with snow piling against the windows.

News came of crowds surging in the dark, snow-piled streets; food giving out, with paralyzed transportation; news of raids by the public upon all the markets; news of people trampled to death hourly at every steamship dock, every bridge leading out of the city; uncontrollable crowds at the tunnels, the railroad and plane terminals.

State troopers vainly patrolled streets made almost impassable by snow which now could not be cleared away; people froze in the cold with which they were not equipped to cope; crime was everywhere, with criminals, like ghouls, battening on tragedy.

In those terrible days there were few concerned with astronomy. Yet I recall that one of my orders was to detail —for any who might still be listening—a simple version of how, astronomically, all this was coming to pass.

29

"Perhaps," I broadcasted, "when we know the fundamentals of this change—the scientific reasons for it—the thing may hold less terror for us."

Useless words! Nothing could mitigate the terror!

"You all know in a general way," I went on, "the astronomical reasons for our alternating day and night—our succession of seasons, spring, summer, autumn and winter. Yet if you follow me closely now, and picture what I tell you, the subject will be clearer to your mind, and you will understand the change which is now upon us. Some of you, our government had advised, should remain in the north and withstand the rigors of the new climate. New York City will not be abandoned! That is absurd! It is the sudden change, the upset to our normal routine, which has now caused suffering.

"When we are equipped for the new conditions, New York and other cities in its latitude will be perfectly habitable. We will have winter nights several months long, and an arctic cold. Then spring, and a summer with the sun giving us months of unending daylight. Those must be our productive months—we must grow food then to supply the southern hemisphere, just as in the other months they must grow food down there.

"Don't be too hasty! We can't all—everyone on Earth —rush at once to the Equator! Even there at times it will be too hot, and a twilight winter fairly cold. Cold enough, a month or two from now, to disorganize everything.

"It is your panic, your haste, which is our greatest danger. Be calm! Meet the conditions as they are. Help our government to maintain order, here in the north. The world's work must be done—the new conditions must be coped with sanely. We are not in desperate distress; only through panic can real disaster come!"

Futile words! But it was the panic of flight—the attempted rush of so many millions of people—the disorganization of all those myriad activities upon which life depends—which was our greatest danger.

Futile words! Impotent governments, themselves disingenuous, for they were all preparing for hasty flight to warmer, more equable regions! On February 22 the National Capital of the United States was moved from Washington, District of Columbia, to temporary housing in Miami, Florida. And even there, the great Florida city was disorganized, snow-covered, with very nearly zero temperature.

The deaths throughout the northern hemisphere that February of 1967 will never be counted. A million? Many million? I would hesitate to guess.

There were some nine million people within the limits of Greater New York on Christmas. By mid-February I suppose there were no more than a scant fifty thousand left—and these, most of them, were trying to get away. A dark, almost deserted, buried city—buried in a white shroud which mercifully hid its tragedy.

I caught one last glimpse of the sun, on the only clear day of that month—the sun at noon just creeping above the southern horizon and then plunging back. The Arctic night was on us.

I saw the highways between New York and Washington, where refugees trudged along on foot, carrying lights in the darkness—plunging through the snow, walking blindly southward when they could go no other way, hundreds falling by the roadside. All the traffic lines were littered with frozen bodies, soon hidden by the snow.

We were not in Washington long; soon we were ordered to Miami. There was a cold gray twilight there which, with the buildings arranged for temporary heating, was at least tolerable. And here we set up our headquarters. The first of March came. Father was in Puerto Rico. I knew by then what strange things were transpiring there in the Cains' plantation house.

I knew, too, what the astronomers—gathered now at Quito, Ecuador, as the best place in the Western World for twilight observation—had discovered.

Xenephrene was inhabited!

Father was convinced of it the day after that momentous February 10. But the news—and the news from the secluded little plantation house of the Cains—was withheld from the public. But on March 2, everything was disclosed. For-

31

our distracted world one culminating blow remained. As though all that had gone before were not enough, fate held one crowning terror.

On March 2 it was broadcast that a hostile race of people in human form had come from Xenephrene and landed on the Earth! Invaders from this brand new world had landed two days before, north of New York, and now were moving south upon the city!

IV

ZETTA

THAT MIDNIGHT of February 10th, Hulda and Dan stood on the small Puerto Rican trail, facing at a brief distance the white girl in the moonlight. She answered Hulda's call. In a queerly small voice her words came to them:

"Zetta! Zetta! Zetta!"

There was a brief silence. Dan murmured, "Let's go nearer."

Slowly, carefully they advanced, fearful of again frightening her. But this time she did not move. She stood watching, trembling slightly, but held her ground. And presently they were confronting her. She was shorter even than Hulda; very slim and frail. A young girl just reaching maturity. A rose, not yet full-blown, Dan thought. But the comparison was wrong. Not a rose, for this was a flower of young womanhood of a species no one of Earth could name.

She seemed, aside from her snow-white hair, no more than a strangely beautiful girl of Earth. But to both Dan and Hulda came again, more strongly than before, the feeling of her strangeness. There was something singularly unusual in her aspect. And as they stood there for a silent instant confronting her, both were conscious of sensations indescribable, as though they were feeling something within themselves—something vague, elusive—something no mortal

32

of Earth had ever felt before. And, perhaps, hearing something—so faint, so ethereal they could not define it—faint as though it were sound heard not by their ears, but by their minds.

And they saw something too, which perhaps no mortal eyes had ever seen before. An aura, a dim, very faint red radiance shone around the three of them as they stood there together in the moonlight.

They stood for a moment, stricken with wonder at their sensations; and perhaps the girl was less timorous as she saw their attitude of awe. She stared up into Dan's face and smiled. Strangely wistful, trusting. A gentle little creature! And he stared down into her dark eyes and found them shimmering pools of iridescence. Then again she spoke, other words in a strange, liquid tongue, soft, with curiously clipped, intoned syllables.

Dan shook his head. "We can't understand you. Can you understand us?"

The girl was waving a hand with what they took to be a gesture of negation. She could not understand their language; and when Dan, realizing it was futile, tried Spanish and then his imperfect French, her gesture continued.

He tried again. "Dan! Dan! Dan!" he said, and struck his chest. And Hulda indicated herself with "Hulda! Hulda!"

The girl's eager face brightened; they had established communication. She cried, "Zetta, Zetta," and laid a hand on her breast.

It was the first communication between the worlds. What dire events, tragedies, amazing things to transpire before the last communication was over!

The girl was persuaded to follow Dan and Hulda, and through all that February she lived with the Cains in the plantation house, guarded and kept hidden, though the news of her presence could not be kept entirely secret.

The silver ball in the coconut grove was a vehicle in which, by some method unknown to Earth, the girl Zetta had come from her world to ours. And she had not come alone. A man had come with her—he seemed to be of middle age. He lay dead near the vehicle. Perhaps the victim of an accident; or perhaps the girl had killed him.

There was no one as yet to say. Zetta could not, apparently, understand any Earth language; and her language seemed hopeless to fathom. She seemed intelligent, docile, willing and anxious to be kept with the Cains; eager, it seemed, to be in the room with them and hear them talk.

Astronomers at Quito had seen the girl's silver vehicle enter the Earth's atmosphere that night of February 10th; and had seen another, infinitely larger. But, almost at once, they lost sight of them. Not there, nor from any of our multitudinous outposts, could this phenomena be traced or tracked down!

Dan notified father of his strange visitor, of course. Father sent instructions. The authorities of Puerto Rico buried the man's body and set a guard to watch constantly over the vehicle as it lay in the grove. Scientists came to inspect it but could understand its mechanism only vaguely.

Two weeks passed. Father was in Miami then; and near the end of February he started by government plane for Puerto Rico.

Conditions all over the world were far worse now. We had only a vague picture. Television and radio were operating intermittently—but all the regular channels for the dissemination of news were paralyzed. And too, the governments withheld, or distorted to a less terrible aspect, such reports as were available.

Europe was enveloped in snow to the Mediterranean; the Barbary Coast was jammed with refugees. London and Paris, like New York, were threatened with complete abandonment.

In Canada, as in Scandinavia, north interior Europe and Asia of the far north, there was less panic, less disaster. There people were accustomed to intense cold and equipped to withstand it.

In the Canadian rural district, the farmers shut themselves up with their winter fundamentals of food as had been their custom, and were said to be making out fairly well. But the big centers of population, dependent upon transportation and industry, were devastated. Greater Montreal was abandoned in February.

Transportation everywhere in the United States was uncertain, chaotic. The new Arctic planes, recently developed, were being hastily manufactured in quantity and were as hastily put into service to carry the people southward. The railroads of our northern states had kept open for a while with snow plows loaned by the great Canadian trunk lines which had long since succumbed.

Steamship service along the Atlantic Coast ventured no farther north than Charleston, South Carolina. The North Atlantic was filled with ice floes driven south by the constant storms. The Polar ice field was reported now as extending nearly down to the former New York-Liverpool steamship lanes.

The St. Lawrence River was frozen solid, from Montreal past Quebec, and down to its mouth, before Christmas. In January the middle Mississippi was solid with an ice bridge which one day snapped and broke, sweeping away three railroad bridges. The Hudson, from Troy to New York harbor, was solid by mid-February. Within a week after that even the Savannah River became impassable, and the port closed.

Yet, for all that, by whatever desperate means possible, great numbers of people were being transported south, and were cared for in their new locations, in the best fashion that could be managed.

What formerly had been our tropic zone was thronged with new arrivals. Daily they poured in from the north. And from the far south, as well—in spite of government's pleadings and commands to the contrary. From Buenos Aires, Rio, Santiago, people were striving to get north, nearer the Equator, fearful of this new heat and blazing daylight which was coming upon them.

Nor was it only a disturbance of the world's normal temperatures. With the abnormal climate came other inevitable disturbances. From widely divergent localities, devastating windstorms were reported. A typhoon, wholly out of season, swept the China Sea. There was a hurricane in

Central America. From Peru and Chile they told us about heavy rains flooding the arid coast. Rain fell at Biskra with torrential rain storms sweeping up and across the Sahara.

The two weeks previous to father's arrival in Puerto Rico were weeks of amazement and awe as Dan and Hulda were brought into closer contact with their beautiful, unearthly visitor.

It came upon them gradually, the strangeness, the weirdness of this girl so like themselves at first glance, yet obviously a being wholly different. They treated her as a guest, though in reality she was a captive. Upon father's advice, the Cains were content to do nothing with Zetta beyond making her one of the family. This seemed to be what she herself desired.

She had her own room next to Hulda's. But she was never in it save to sleep. Eagerly and persistently, she listened to every word spoken. To learn our language appeared to be her sole interest.

To Dan, her constant presence was at once fascinating and disturbing. Fascinating, for Zetta's beauty was definitely magnetic. But disturbing too, for there was about this girl that something *different*, indefinable.

For hours she would sit in the living room, apart from the family group. She did not like the chairs, preferring to sit cross-legged on the floor on a cushion. She was silent, following our converstation with a smile or strange little gesture. Her eyes never left the lips of the person speaking.

Her complexion was the creamy, pink-white which we of Earth call beauty. She seemed to blush readily. A wave of rose color would suffuse her face, throat and neck, even extending sometimes to her arms, and to her legs as they showed amid her half-revealing drapery—the smooth white of her skin flushing with deep rose color. For no reason—then Dan noticed that it generally happened when the outer door was opened and a rush of cold air swept in. Nature automatically protecting against the cold!

Dan often would furtively watch her. He was sitting in a

far corner of the room one evening. The elder Cains and Hulda were gathered about the television.

The small clear voice of the announcer was giving a summary of the world's tragic plight, this middle of February. On the screen, flitting, distorted pictures, sometimes gaining rational form, were mirrored.

Zetta was seated on the floor, in an opposite corner from Dan. He saw that she was not listening to the announcer. But she was listening to something! Her head was tilted, alert; across her face a succession of her emotions was mirrored: a frown; whimsical pleasure; a smile.

She was listening; and Dan realized suddenly that she was hearing things he could not hear! A world of things, perhaps. Something displeased her; she gestured disapprovingly. And then smiled again.

Uncanny! She was wholly absorbed, unaware that Don was watching her. Hearing things that no mortal of Earth could hear! Like a dog, Dan thought, which hears faint sounds denied its master. But Dan knew it was more than that.

And then his heart leaped. Zetta was seeing something he could not see! Something in the room. Her eyes followed it, as evidently it moved. She turned her head to gaze after it; she smiled, with breathless parted lips, then laughed.

Was she, perhaps, irrational? Conjuring visions in an unbalanced mind? This explanation occurred to Dan, but he did not believe it was so. Rather, it seemed to him, this girl's preceptions were more acute than ours.

She saw and heard things beyond the range of our human senses. Here on Earth they were things strange to her. She was listening and watching them; surprised, often pleased, as one with normal senses gazes upon new sights and finds them interesting.

Dan found opportunity to regard the girl more closely. Her eyes, when she looked at him, seemed normal. But at other times he saw that her pupils became suddenly abnormally large; or again, contracted to pinpoints, even in the dimness of indoors. At once, a dark veil, a film, seemed to

37

creep over her eyes. But she became aware of the scrutiny, and it was gone before Dan could make sure.

Her ears, in outward shape a trifle rounder than ours, were generally hidden in the waving mass of white hair. Dan fancied that they moved at her will, that sometimes they expanded. Her fingers, and her toes, were long, slim and tapering, with pink-white pointed nails. The joints were more numerous than with us: it gave them a prehensile aspect. And Dan fancied, too, that the arch of the bottom of her foot was cup-shaped as though it might serve as a vacuum for walking upon inclined surfaces.

Father had told Dan that Zetta probably was from Xenephrene. But no one could be sure. An idea occurred to Dan a few days later, just before dawn, and he and Hulda tried it. Xenephrene, on clear days, was visible just before sunrise. The weather here in Puerto Rico was now generally below freezing. The Cains' fruit trees had been killed by the cold. But with all the world's catastrophe for comparison, Dan and his father thought little of it. The Puerto Rican day now was but two hours long. The sun made a low arc in the south and descended not very much to the west of where it had risen.

It was mid morning when in the darkness before dawn, Hulda and Dan stood with Zetta outside the plantation house. To the south Xenephrene would soon rise.

"Do you think she'll recognize it?" Hulda asked.

Dan smiled. How could one guess? Zetta stood between them, puzzled, looking first at one, then at the other. She had walked out with them quietly. She always walked quietly, carefully, as though trying to imitate their steps. And though Dan, with gestures, had often tried to make her leap into the air, she never would.

It was cold, this mid morning before dawn. Dan and Hulda were dressed in heavy, northern garments. Zetta wore the filmy robe in which they had first seen her. She seemed to prefer her own garments, a number of which had been brought from the vehicle and installed with her at the Cains'. She appeared to be utterly oblivious of the cold of outdoors, or the warmth inside.

38

They stood on the knoll. The sky to the southward was brightening. The stars there moved in a low arc. Then Xenephrene came up, a blazing, purple-white star.

"Look!" said Dan. "Zetta, look! We call that Xenephrene. Can't you understand me? Do you recognize that star? Your world? Did you come from there?"

At sight of the great purple star, an emotion swept her face.

Dan pleaded, "Zetta, haven't you learned anything of our language? We've all tried so hard to make you understand it, to help you learn it! We call that Planet Xenephrene. Your world? You came from there? Speak, Zetta!"

She said slowly in English, with an accent quaint and indescribable: "Yes. My worl'. I came from there."

"But what's the matter with you, Hulda?"

"Nothing."

"But there is!"

"Not at all, Dan. Why do you say that?"

"But there is! You're angry, or hurt. At me? What have I done?"

"Nonsense. You haven't done—" She stopped; and he saw that her eyes were filled with sudden tears. She tried to protest but the words would not come.

They were sitting alone late one evening in the Cains' living room. Dan had noticed that for some days Hulda had been abnormally quiet; and she no longer treated him with her usual warmth. A reserve had come to her. And now, when he asked her why, she burst into tears!

She sobbed openly. He tried to put his arm around her, but she pushed him away.

"Hulda!" A light broke on Dan. "It's Zetta—why, you silly little girl—"

"You were—were kissing her this morning!"

"I was *not!* That's nonsense!"

"Well, I s-saw you, with her in your arms, l-lifting her up—"

"Yes. Lifting her up. But not kissing her. But I'm kissing *you!* Now—like that! And *that*—Hulda darling—"

It is not my part to reconstruct the scene that followed between them, although both have described the wonder of it to all of the family who would listen—wonder and awe at the voicing of love which all of us knew they had felt for each other the last couple of years. They were engaged when ten minutes later they thumped on the elder Cains' door to tell them the wonderful news.

Dan maintained that to Zetta he owed a great debt of gratitude, for without Hulda's jealousy of Zetta, Dan says he might have been too stupid to have proposed at that time. The episode with Zetta was simple enough: Dan explained it readily to Hulda's entire satisfaction.

He had been alone with Zetta that morning, trying to make her talk more of our language which now he knew she was learning. With a mind wholly different than ours—this Dan now realized—she was undoubtedly absorbing with extraordinary rapidity. But, quite evidently, she had her own method. She would not speak again. But when he began naming objects in the room, trying to aid her by systematic teaching, she showed approval and listened attentively.

During the course of this lesson, Dan had touched her arm. He laid his hand on her arm. Curious sensation. He felt at once, not a lack of solidity, but a seeming lack of weight. She had risen to her feet as though startled by his touch. He stood, from his much greater height looking down at her, still holding her arm.

And this Dan confessed to me, but most assuredly he did not confess it to Hulda. As he stood there, staring into the glowing dark depths of Zetta's eyes, it occurred to him that he should release her. But he did not. Instead, he caught her in his arms, and lifted her up. Not, to be wholly truthful, because scientifically he wanted to test her weight. Rather was it because, at touching her, an instant of madness swept him.

It passed. She was pushing him away, smiling, startled but unafraid. And, with the madness gone, he tossed her into the air as one would toss a young child. Caught her; tossed her again to the ceiling and let her fall, to land lightly on tiptoe as her feet came down to the straw matting on the floor. And in the doorway, he became aware that Hulda was standing, silently watching them.

When father arrived at the Cains', he weighed Zetta. Had she been a normal girl of Earth, by her appearance she would have weighed some ninety or a hundred pounds. Zetta weighed eighteen pounds!

There were several scientists in Puerto Rico who, at father's invitation, came to see Zetta. They were with her hours each day. Dan and Hulda were excluded. Father's manner, Dan said, was increasingly solemn during this period and he seemed to be laboring under a suppressed excitement or alarm.

Then came the news of March 2, that invaders from Xenephrene had landed on Earth near New York. The scientists at the Cains' house hastened to San Juan, but father remained.

One afternoon—it was the afternoon of March 4—Hulda and Dan listened at the door when father was with Zetta. She was talking to him now! Talking in low, slow tones, haltingly, and often he would question and prompt her.

Abruptly the door opened and he came out, highly excited.

"Hulda! Oh, Dan, where are your father and mother?"

Dan called them. They came hustling in. The pace of these days was too much for the elder Cains: they lived in a constant confusion and bewilderment.

"Sit down. All of you," father said hurriedly. "Zetta—come out here, child."

She came at his call, wide-eyed, gentle. But she too was trembling with excitement. Father seated her gently on a cushion. He said:

"No matter how much turmoil has been caused by the frightening changes in the Earth's climate, I'm afraid the total situation is far worse off than that. Zetta you see her as a calm, unperturbed young girl—but this is the exterior, only. Within her has been the desperate need to learn our language, to gain the ability to transmit to us a warning. These invaders—well, what Zetta can now tell us will at

41

least give us information—aid us in doing what we can to repel them! It is a bad condition—it may prove serious—possibly complete disaster!"

He regarded Zetta with a gentle tenderness. "This girl has come from her world with the sole purpose of helping us. Yes, she, with that one aim, day in and day out, has learned our language, with what strange qualities of mind, and senses so different from ours, you will be amazed to hear. A very gentle little creature. I think all of you have learned to love her. She says you have been very kind to her, and she loves you very much, particularly Hulda."

It struck Hulda with a guilty pang, hearing this after her own jealousy of Zetta; for Hulda was no more than human, and there had been days when secretly she hotly resented the strange and beautiful girl's presence in the house with Dan. But that was over. Hulda exclaimed impulsively, "I do love her!"

The two girls' glances met affectionately. "Yes," Zetta said firmly. "We do love ver' much."

Father raised a hand. "Let's hear from Zetta. Tell them child—just what you told me."

Father stopped his nervous pacing and sat down abruptly. And without preface, quietly, sometimes haltingly, in her strangely small voice and curiously clipped syllables, Zetta began her amazing narrative.

V

CRIMSON SOUND

ON THE AFTERNOON of March 3, Freddie and I, in Miami, were summoned by the War Department, which was installed there in makeshift fashion after its haphazard flight from Washington. We were greeted by the secretary, who introduced us to a dozen or more grave-faced officials who were seated around a large table in a cold, badly illumined room. They were under the impression that I had recently been to Puerto Rico with my father; they wanted further details from me, as an eyewitness, to supplement the sketchy information which had been furnished them concerning the captive girl from Xenephrene.

I had not been to Puerto Rico, so I could tell them nothing, but I remained at the conference with Freddie. Of him, they wanted a demonstration of his invention. The War Secretary laughed, but it was a very hollow, mirthless laugh.

"You see, young man, we're almost in the position of grasping at straws."

The inner workings of a government are never understood by the general public, which reads of war conferences and grave official decisions given with calm dignity in times of national crisis. The people naturally picture men of great intellect, calmly, judiciously weighing problems of procedure and quietly giving their decisions, as though the whole matter were controlled by some giant, insensate machine of precision, incapable of error, undisturbed by human emotion.

It is not so. Or, at least, I can vouch for the fact that in the darkness of this afternoon of March 3, in the United States War Department at Miami, it most certainly was not so.

These anxious men were very human. Most were unshaven, with rumpled hair and reddened eyes. Distraught, harassed, undecided, doubtful of every move: striving to do the best they could, with the welfare of millions at stake. Conditions of unprecedented disaster had for weeks assailed them. Under this culminating blow—invaders from another world landing to attack what was once our greatest city— and with communication at its lowest ebb—they were all but broken.

Very human indeed! The Secretary of Navy sat savagely chewing on the stump of an old cigar, blowing on his hands, cursing the cold at intervals. The Air Secretary was pouring hot coffee at the end of the table, shoving a litter of papers out of his way to make room for the cups. The stooped, middle-aged, haggard gentleman pacing the floor was our President.

"Grasping at a straw," said the War Secretary.

In a sudden silence, through an open doorway to the room adjoining, I could hear the clatter of telephone bells, the hiss and splutter of the radio and television instruments.

"Close that door," the secretary added querulously. Then he added, "You've brought your model, Smith? Put it here on the table—tell us about it."

Freddie opened his apparatus and explained it briefly. His so-called thermodyne principle. Though ultimately he had hoped to adapt it into a motor of revolutionary design, his present model was merely a small projector.

"Projector of what?" demanded the President irritably.

"Of heat, sir," Freddie answered. "I'll show you. This is a very small model, of course, but it demonstrates the principle."

They did not want any technicalities from Freddie. He explained only that his apparatus, in this present small form, took a tiny electric spark and built it up into a new form of radiant heat.

"It is," said Freddie, "heat of totally different properties from the kind with which we commonly deal. It travels—radiates, by the diffusion of its electrons—more like light than heat. At a great speed—I think possibly at over a hundred thousand miles a second."

He opened his apparatus. It consisted of a small, flat, metallic box, curved to fit a man's chest. A disk, like a small electrode, to be pressed against the skin. Freddie bared his chest and strapped it on.

"I use the tiny electrical impulse which the human body itself furnishes. This I amplify, build up and store in a battery." Wires from the generator led to a small box which Freddie opened to show his audience—a box of coils, and a tiny row of amplifying tubes. He put this in his pocket, with wires leading to the battery and projector. These were both in one piece—the projector a small metallic funnel, with a trigger; and a grid of wires was across its opened end. It had a long metallic handle, in the hollow interior of

44

which was the battery where the charge was concentrated.

"Electrons of heat under pressure," said Freddie.

"Show us," said someone.

Freddie erected a screen across the room—an insulating screen to kill the heat-beam so that it could not injure the wall. The men moved aside.

Freddie, after a moment to generate and concentrate the charge, raised the muzzle.

The thing hissed slightly; a dull violet beam sprang like a light from the projector. It struck the screen some twenty feet away, in a large circle of fluorescence; in the dimness of the room it seemed like phosphorescent water, landing in a spray and dissipating as it struck, like a dissolving mist.

Freddie cried, "Peter, hold something in it!"

I took a sheet of paper, held it carefully into the beam. It shriveled, blackened and burst into flame. Then a lead pencil—it melted off midway of its length as I held it up.

Freddie snapped off the apparatus. "That's all, gentlemen. With a large model, I would use a high voltage current for my original impulse instead of the tiny impulse of the human body."

"How far will that beam carry?" the President demanded.

"This one?" Freddie asked. "Or a maximum, full-sized projector?"

"This one. Why talk about what you haven't got?"

"About thirty-five feet, sir. Further, perhaps, if I concentrate it—keep it from spreading. Say fifty feet. But at that distance its temperature would not be very great."

"How great?"

"Two hundred degrees Fahrenheit."

"How much is it at the muzzle?"

"About twelve hundred."

An effective range of thirty-five or fifty feet! They were all disappointed. The man beside me said, "This thing is useless to help us now, gentlemen. But in the future—do you know, I wouldn't say but that this young fellow has hit upon something not unlike what our enemies seem to be using—"

45

The door from the adjoining room opened. A man said, "Davis has started his flight. He's almost within sight of them now—shall I bring in the screen? It's murky and distorted, but—"

"Bring it in," said the President. "Get these lights lowered —put that away, Mr. Smith; we'll discuss it further some other time. It has been very interesting."

Freddie hastily gathered up his apparatus. The lights in the conference room were turned out; it was illumined only by the blue reflection through the doorway. Men brought in a television with a screen some two feet square and placed it on the table. We all gathered before it. The instrument room door was closed. We were in the darkness save for the vague silver radiance shot with strokes of vivid light that came from the screen.

From the whispers around me I soon knew what was transpiring. The invaders had landed on the east bank of the frozen Hudson, near the suburb of Tarrytown. Xenephrene was at its closest point to Earth now, which was what doubtless prompted the invasion. Xenephrene was passing us: beginning today, the distance between the worlds would grow greater.

Presumably the invaders had landed on the night of February 28. It had been snowing around New York City steadily for a week, but that night had been clear. Reports said that a great silver ball had been seen floating down from the sky. Later, from the ground, strange beams of colored light were seen, moving slowly southward. And strange sounds were heard.

But the information was confused and unauthentic. This last blizzard had cut off all the New York area from the world. There was practically no transportation of any kind; no wires remained standing; no radio or television stations were operating within all that region.

How many people remained on Manhattan Island, no one could say. Very few, probably. A deserted, congealed city, snow-buried, with its huge buildings nothing now but giant monuments to a greatness that once had been. The cold was worse than the scientists had prognosticated. Nothing could get to New York now save possibly dog-sleds, and the new type Arctic planes—and very few of those were available.

War against the invaders from Xenephrene!

Our government bulletins of the day had assured the public that these invaders would be held in check, attacked, held from moving further south and very soon exterminated. What deaths to our people they had already caused, was not known. But it was evident that they were hostile; a plane carrying refugees had passed near their lights. Confused stories were told of melting, vanishing snow under red light; and stories of another refugee plane attacked and destroyed by red light and strange sound! Meaningless news! Yet terrible!

What was left of the British Empire, from its capital in North Africa, offered us aid. They were building the Arctic planes. The French government from its headquarters in Tunis, preparing to move again south to the lower Sahara, got through its radioed message to offer help. Argentina and Chile, harassed with their own problems in the new tropic heat, wanted to help if they could.

Magnificent gestures, but they all meant very little. So far, nothing had been done. A few of our planes had ventured near New York; and none had so far been heard from since. Now, a huge Arctic plane, commanded by this Davis, equipped with modern aircraft artillery, with many of the weapons of modern science, was making an experimental flight. A companion plane, flown by the famous Robinson, was with it. Robinson had the longest range missile of modern times. His purpose was to try to get above the enemy; and Davis, with his sending equipment, would report conditions as best he could.

The attempt then, was what now we were to witness. I have never been present at so dramatic a scene as this one which took place on the screen and in the room around me.

In the darkness the silver light from the screen vaguely illumined the tense crowding figures. The highest officials of our government!

No calm judicial conference here! Tired, cold, anxious

47

men, watching and listening with bated breaths and thumping hearts. There had been a buzz of whispered comments; the shifting of chairs; shuffling of feet. But now there was silence.

The screen image blurred for a moment, but soon it was comparatively clear. I was able to see the cold, frosty stars in a field of blue-black; far below, the dim vista of gray-white snow shining in the starlight—a panorama of snow-laden country at night. The image finder was in the front of Davis' plane, pointing diagonally downward. A swaying scene, shot with streaks of dazzling light.

Someone said, "Where are we? I don't recognize that landscape."

"Long Island. He's heading for New York City. Quiet! We'll throw in his radio-sound." It was the voice of the War Secretary. "Grant, you said you had connection."

A man was fumbling with the miniature audiophone beside the mirror. We heard the drone of Davis' plane; and then his voice, with words indistinguishable through the static as he spoke to the gunner beside him.

The President said nervously, "Have you sending connection? If we want to give him orders—where is the other plane? Isn't Robinson close by?"

Grant said, "Yes. He was visible a while ago. Davis is going to fly over New York—he thinks the enemy is still up in the Tarrytown or Yonkers district."

I sat staring at the screen. Half an hour? Or two hours? I could not have said. Swaying stars. A dim white swaying landscape. Then the horizon dropped; stars covered everything; Davis was mounting. He leveled at last.

Dimly, far down, I could see the white configurations of Long Island Sound, frozen into solid ice, white with piled snow drifts, black in small patches where the wind had swept it bare. A blurred, shifting scene, dizzying, but sometimes steady and surprisingly clear. It tilted up—all land for a moment.

I saw momentarily, as the plane swooped down, the great bridges over the river from Long Island to Manhattan. Small as a child's toys. Broken toy bridges, with ice piled

48

upon them, cables dangling. The older Brooklyn Bridge lay askew. A jam of river ice had wrenched at one of its ends.

It was a motionless world: the river of tangled, motionless ice-floes, the frozen, motionless bay with hulks of vessels caught in it and abandoned. And the great city—all congealed, stricken of motion in every detail.

And then we were over lower New York. The parks were wan, white blobs, the streets like deep black canyons; the great buildings in the crowded financial district stood like frozen headstones. Davis swooped—I saw a great office building in which the water system must have burst and flooded it when there was still warmth inside: its facade was a mass of ice. The plane zoomed up and only the stars were visible.

Above the motor drone from the autiophone, the President's voice said, "Ask him about Robinson. Where is he?"

Then we saw Robinson's large quadruplane with its helicopters folded, its cabin hanging like a silver bullet beneath the lower wing. It came swinging into our image from one side, and headed north into the starlight.

Abruptly we heard Davis's voice: "Above Central Park. It's piled level as an Arctic snow-field. In the lower city there didn't seem to be any lights—saw no signs of anyone remaining. The enemy is in the open country up ahead, northeast of the Yonkers district—look! There now, you see the enemy light!"

At the distant northern horizon in the background of the image, a dull radiance of red was visible. It seemed a crimson glow standing up into the sky. Not the yellow of a reflected conflagration, but red—crimson red.

"Blood!" murmured the man beside me. "Crimson stain—"

Davis's voice was saying, "I'll keep in sight of Robinson. He's mounting. I'm cutting out my connection with you now, except the image and the continuing one-way sound. You'll hear and see better. Hear and see all that we do—I can begin to hear—Goodby to you all."

His voice broke with a snap that indicated his connection was off.

The War Secretary cried, "Grant! Stop him! We must

49

be able to talk with him—give him orders—warnings! That fool daredevil, he's likely to do anything just to make it easier for us to see and hear more!"

But the connection was broken. Davis, with that ominous, significant "Goodby to you all," had cut out.

The mirror was brighter and clearer with its greater power; the drone of the plane came louder, and then dimmed suddenly as Davis evidently threw in his mufflers.

In the silence now, we heard another sound. The sound of the enemy! The sound of that crimson radiance in the sky overhead! A low whine. It did not seem electrical. A whine—more like a giant animal in distress.

I listened, with a shudder filling me; and I know that every man in the room must have felt the same. A queer thrilling shudder, as though the very sound itself were physically affecting me with its vibrations. It was very soft, now at first, and I was only hearing the faint, radio echo of it. Yet upon my senses it laid a singularly weird, uncanny feeling of the diabolical.

The minutes passed. As the plane flew northward, the crimson stain in the sky seemed spreading. And the whine increased; grew louder, resolved itself now into a myriad undertones. Cries, muffled, faint, aerial, yet somehow clear; screams, checked and then begun again; a low, tiny throbbing—a myriad unearthly sounds, weirdly abnormal, like nothing I had ever heard before, all blended as undertones to the one great whine.

The crimson radiance, screaming into the night! Light and sound intermingled. Was this some weapon of a strange science which the invaders from Xenephrene had brought to attack us? There was something deadly in the aspect of that crimson radiance—and something equally lethal in the gruesome sound which split the night around it.

My thoughts were whirling in this fashion when I heard the muttered words of the man next to me, murmuring to the man on his other side:

"That's weird! Vanderstuyft says that the girl from Xenephrene can see and hear below the human scale! This

50

is it—the infrared made visible, and its sounds brought up to our human ears! Weird—"

Some one else was asking, "Is that light and that sound their weapon? Where's the Robinson plane?"

And the War Secretary said, "Quiet! He's there—ahead. Mounting."

Nothing but sky again. A blood-red night sky. The stars gleamed like crimson jewels through the radiance. Then again the Davis plane leveled. We saw now that the invaders evidently were encamped in a snowy stretch of what had been comparatively open country. The houses which once were there lay now under mounds of snow. A blank rolling landscape; fences, roads all gone beneath the billowing blanket of white. Only the trees were left: stark, black sticks in patches.

In an oval, perhaps a mile across its greatest diameter, the red beam stood up into the sky, a barrage of crimson. It throbbed and screamed and whined its defiance!

The two planes circled the radiance, some ten thousand feet up, and several miles away. The Davis plane fired a shell; we heard the dull, muffled report, saw a yellow glare where it struck the red beam and harmlessly exploded. But it struck low, where perhaps the sound vibrations were too intense.

The planes mounted higher. We could see Robinson's ahead and above us! He was closer to the crimson barrage. Trying to fly directly over it—to drop a bomb and make a direct hit, very probably.

From this greater height, within the oval, other lights showed far down on the snow. Tiny moving spots of vivid color. The enemy's encampment.

Davis was now at least at the twenty thousand foot level. Robinson was still higher. In that deadly cold, it seemed incredible. But still they struggled up.

At this height the crimson barrage was thin. Once, overhead, I seemed to see where it ended. The whine of it was fainter, but every gruesome undertone still sounded clear.

"He's trying it!" The man beside me blurted it out aloud.

Startled movement sounded in the room. A chair pushed back with a rasp. Tense murmurs. Shuffling feet. We stared. Robinson's plane darted in—

There was just an instant when I thought it was safely through. I could see it clearly—the black outline of a bird stained crimson. It seemed to hang motionless, then it fluttered, falling—and as it fell, like a mist of black vapor it suddenly expanded: a black wraith of a plane expanding, dissipating. It did not seem to reach the ground. It was gone, dissolved into nothing visible, with only a howling, mouthing sound from the crimson monster to mark its passing!

A shiver swept me. I was cold, trembling. I heard someone near me cry in horror; "Davis, he's—" and then check himself.

The screen was a blur of crimson, with lurid spots of light on the ground showing through it. Davis was heading downward in a swoop through the red beam! It spread until the whole image before us was a crimson stain.

The lights on the ground seemed to be leaping up, growing in size as the plane dived at them. The room was a chaos of gruesome tiny screams! We were in the crimson! It snapped with a myriad sparks. It howled, squealed, screamed! An instant, but it seemed an eternity. Then the red vanished. We were through it—by Heaven, through it! Diving at the ground!

I saw that one of the spots of light had broadened to a green, ghastly glare on the snow surface. Figures of men in human form stood there, foreshortened by the overhead perspective to huge heads and dwindling bodies. Human forms: men of almost naked bodies, standing in the snow, bodies painted green with the glare. Apparatus of war erected in the snow—a bare spot where the snow was gone, and rock and earth showed clean—a shimmer that seemed a pool of water lying warm with ice around it.

A glimpse, no more than a second or two. Then the scene, rushing upward, was fading. The confusion of sounds and blurred lights suddenly grew faint—faded—vanished into darkness and silence!

The screen was dead, a blank silver surface staring at us like a corpse. The audiophone was mute.

Davis's plane had vanished like its fellow into nothingness before it reached the ground!

This was the afternoon of March 3. That night, while Freddie and I were at the boarding place, the news reached us that a silver ball of invaders from Xenephrene had landed in the twilight of the Venezuelan coast—the heart of the region which in all our western hemisphere we had come to prize most dearly!

VI

"IF I HAD KNOWN"

"LOOK HERE, young man," said the War Secretary, "can you operate a plane of the Arctic A type?"

I could, and so could Freddie, I said. The War Secretary continued his pacing of the room. It was about nine o'clock of the morning of March 15—black as midnight outdoors: cold, with clouds scurrying low over the Florida Keys, clouds which promised snow. The War Secretary had sent for us.

Conditions were worse everywhere, it seemed now by this morning's news—as though each day brought disasters worse than any which had gone before. The invaders from Xenephrene were obviously almost impregnable to our attack. The efforts of Davis and Robinson had proved that, if nothing else. It was obvious also that the invaders at New York City so far had made no offensive move. Their barrage—the crimson howling sound, or light, whatever it might be—was merely their defense.

"Heaven knows," the Secretary exclaimed, "what weapons they may have to loose upon us when they begin an attack!"

And now, another huge ball had landed in Venezuela, on the coastal plain near La Guayra. In the deserted frozen

53

wastes of New York State the invaders were not an immediate, serious menace. But in Venezuela it was a far different condition.

La Guayra was the main receiving port for all our refugee ships. A twilight had fallen there, but the temperature still was mild. It was colder up in Caracas, but the people thronged there, and with heroic efforts the Government and the citizens were doing their best to receive them.

It was not a wholly unselfish effort. With the new climate, Colombia, Venezuela, Ecuador, Peru, the former jungles of the Amazon basin of Brazil, even the mountain fastnesses of Bolivia and the arid coast of north Chile—this was the land of promise. It was the best, the only tolerable all-year climate left to the Western World. Here the new great cities would spring up, centers of industry and commerce; here would be the new great fields of grain, the cattle ranges.

But here, in the midst of the confusion of arriving settlers, the enemy from Xenephrene had landed! We had no details. We knew only that around the silver ball a barrage of red howling sound was standing up into the sky. Within the circular mile of that red barrage, all that had been evidence of our human life—houses, trees, people—all was vanished!

The War Secretary stopped before me. "I radioed your father this morning, Peter. Told him to send that Xenephrene girl up here to us at once. We must learn, if we can, what these unearthly enemies are like—do what we can to oppose them."

He gestured at me vehemently. "Your father told me he was very busy—he'd have full information for me in a few days! That's the scientist for you! Taking it methodically, with that damn scientific routine, when a day or two is an eternity just now."

I regarded Freddie. We did not smile. In these terrible days there was not a smile left in us. But Freddie nodded.

I said, "That's father's way. But—"

"Well, I told him I was sending a special plane down there at once to get him and the girl. The Venezuelan government is demanding details of us. Every thirty minutes Caracas calls me up. Makes a fool of us—a girl of this unknown enemy race right in our hands and we don't produce her! Your father said, 'Send Peter and Fred Smith for us—I want to see them anyway'."

There was nothing that could have pleased Freddie and me better. The secretary offered us a pilot, but we did not want one. We started that morning, armed with legal papers given us jocularly but with serious intent nevertheless, and commanding father's presence with Zetta in Miami the next day.

It was eleven o'clock when we got away in the big Arctic A plane. A black morning with swift low clouds, and a wind from the north. Flying southeast, we had scarcely left the Bahamas behind us when the weather cleared. Cold starlight shone on a dark, cold ocean. Icebergs had been seen down this far, but we did not chance to pass any now. We did see many scurrying steamships.

In some four hours we raised the Morrow light of San Juan and I turned southwest, to strike the coast beyond Arecibo. Flying low, we headed in, over the line of breakers on the white beach. Columbus had landed near here, not so many lifetimes ago. Yet how different was the world then!

The tumbled mountains rising behind the sea which Columbus had described to Isabella rose before us now. The same shape: every tiny peak undoubtedly practically the same. But they were not the vivid warm green which had so enchanted the mariner. These were cold and blue-gray, and the tops of them were white with snow.

It was mid-afternoon when, in the darkness, we dropped with a roar upon Dan's landing stage at the foot of the knoll. We leaped from the plane and hurried up the hill, to see Dan and father, and Hulda and the Cains waving at us from the veranda, and a small, strange white figure of a girl standing among them.

If one could only glimpse the future, even for a brief moment! It makes me shudder sometimes to think how blindly we are forced to tread our way through life, raising each foot without the knowledge of what will happen before it reaches the ground! That afternoon, for instance, I was very happy to burst in upon father and Dan. If Freddie and I had known what was impending, we would have done anything rather than arrive at that moment. If we had delayed our arrival even an hour! Yet, even in a seeming tragedy, there is evidence of some all-guiding purpose. We may not see it: but I think that always it is there.

We came upon the plantation house within a moment after Zetta had begun her narration. She had told it to father. She was beginning it for Dan and the others, when the sound of our arriving plane checked her.

The few remaining hours of that afternoon and evening were crowded with the confusion of our arrival, our exchange of news and ideas, and listening to some disjointed world news from the radio. Zetta did not tell her story that afternoon or that evening. Father, with a quizzical smile, looked over the legal papers with which we served him.

"Good enough, boys! I'll obey them. We'll take Zetta and go up to Miami tomorrow morning." He turned to Dan. "You come with us. Zetta will tell her story to the authorities in Miami, just as she's told it to me. And I'll have some helpful and interesting scientific data for them, I promise you. We have not been idle here."

He gestured with a voluminous sheaf of papers—his scientific notes on Zetta's narrative and on the girl's mental and physical being. After gesturing with the papers, he put them back in his pocket. Fate! Call it what you will. He did not hand them to Dan or Freddie, or me. He stuck them back in his pocket!

The news of Hulda's and Dan's engagement brought me pleasure. I shook Dan's hand warmly and kissed my sister as she flung herself into my arms. Little Hulda was radiant. Dan's handsome tanned face was flushed as he received our congratulations; and when they were over, he stood towering over Hulda, with his arms around her as she clung to

56

him—two lovers, snatching at their happiness even in the midst of the world's turmoil.

I shall never forget my meeting with Zetta, as they introduced her to me that afternoon. She stood in the center of the room, and something momentarily diverted the rest of them from us. For an instant we were alone. I stared at her.

What futile words of greeting I may have uttered, I do not know. She said nothing. I saw a quaintly beautiful young girl, curiously different from any girl I had ever beheld. A strange, weird beauty. I took her hand as she held it out in the gesture they had taught her.

I have mentioned Dan's feelings under similar circumstances. Dan was in love with Hulda. The instinct of all that was good and right within him rose, when he was so attracted to Zetta, to cast out this surge of alien emotion. Not so, with me. I was unfettered, wholly fancy free.

I took Zetta's hand. It seemed then as though the contact might at any moment become beyond my power to break. Her gaze held mine. I saw a startled look in her eyes, and then saw something else—the mirrored play of emotions like my own.

Her body seemed to sway toward me. I could see and feel her withstanding its sway, the attraction between us. Do I mean that literally, scientifically? I do not know. There is, perhaps, between the sexes on Earth such an attraction. Or it may be psychological, emotional, nothing more.

I felt it with Zetta, and I could see that she felt it and was startled. But in her eyes there was more than surprise—a swift melting look of tenderness.

Mrs. Cain bustled up to us. "Isn't she a darling little thing, Pete? We all love her. Oh dear, these terrible, strange times!"

Our hands broke apart. Was it love we had felt in that instant? Could love be possible, could it be right between a man and woman so different? Does the Creator intend for the worlds thus to be joined, or is the isolation He had imposed on each of them an evidence that such should not be?

57

Love between Zetta and me? I do not know. But all that afternoon and evening I found my eyes turning to her, and found her somber gaze upon me.

We chanced to approach each other several times, and always I was conscious of the attraction of her nearness. Not so strong as at first. All my instinct, my reason, was prepared for it now; a thousand barriers of conventionality and time and place and circumstance contributed subconsciously to resist it. But it was there, invisibly, intangibly holding us.

The evening's radio news brought a measure of relief to the world. From New York came the report that the invaders had vanished. Moved somewhere else, possibly—but if so, it was not known.

Father made one comment. His words, which proved to be true enough, linger clear in my memory: "They left New York yesterday afternoon, after the attack by Robinson and Davis. There are not two vehicles—only one! It left New York and landed last night in Venezuela. It may leave there presently." His glance turned to Zetta. "I have reason to think that the invaders will voluntarily withdraw from the Earth. Very soon, I imagine—while Xenephrene is still comparatively near us."

True enough! At midnight that night the radio told us that the Xenephrene vehicle, with all its people, had left Venezuela. The night was heavily overcast, with a rain and wind storm all up through Central America and the lower Caribbean; and north of sixteen degrees there was snow. Where the invaders had gone, no one knew. The world was anxiously awaiting news of their next landing place.

We sat up for perhaps an hour. It was snowing outside, with a howling wind that swirled the snow about the eaves of the small plantation house. At about one o'clock we all bade one another goodnight and went to bed.

Ah, if we had known!

I awoke to find Freddie shaking me. He and I had slept together. It was four in the morning, and the house was noisy with the storm outside. Freddie was alarmed—he did not know why. Something had awakened him. We decided it was a thumping which we now heard in the living room, a door banging in the wind, with a queer, broken rattle to it.

There is a sense of evil to anyone awakened unexpectedly in the night. I felt it very strongly now. And Freddie's face was white and solemn in the glow of the night light which he had switched on.

"The door to the porch," I said. "It's blown open—it's banging."

We went out to close it. The living room was very cold; snow was blowing in through the outer doorway. We turned on the light here. The door was not only open, it was hanging askew, half torn from its hinges. More than that, part of its framework was gone. Not broken: vanished, as if melted off. A leprous wreck of a door, hanging there, banging with a thump and rattle in the wind!

No need to tell us what had happened. I think we knew it then. The door to father's bedroom stood open. He was not there. The bed had been occupied; there was no sign of a struggle, no abnormal disorder anywhere about the house, except for that dismembered front door, which had been locked.

Our light and our voices awakened Dan and his parents. They came out from their rooms. But Hulda did not come, nor Zetta! Their bedroom doors, like father's stood open. But the occupants were gone.

Horrified moments followed, during which we searched the house and the buildings near it. There was no evidence of any kind of how, in the noisy night, while the rest of us slept, father, Hulda and Zetta had been spirited away.

The terrified elder Cains remained in the house. Hastily dressing, Dan, Freddie and I rushed to the Corral. The chilled little ponies welcomed us. We saddled, and in single file, slowly against the wind and driving snow, we rode out into the night.

There was no surprise left in us when we reached the "Eden tract" in the valley by the caves where once the Cains' treasured fruit trees had grown so luxuriantly. It was

59

all a dim gray expanse of snow, with the naked tree branches showing in black, forlorn rows.

The trunks of the coconut trees stood like huge black sticks in a patch of white. But among them there was no small silver vehicle. The guards had been withdrawn a week before. There was no evidence here of anything.

The heavy falling snowflakes would have covered up even recent footprints. There was only the depression where the vehicle had stood.

The last communication was broken. The last remaining evidence of Xenephrene upon our Earth was gone!

VII

MYSTERIOUS PLANET, IMPERTURBABLY SHINING!

MORE THAN TWICE seventeen months went by. For me and for Dan the progress of the world, it seemed then, must always be in cycles of seventeen months, the length of time which Xenephrene took periodically to overtake and pass us in our orbit. Almost between us and the sun, every seventeen months; and at such times she was at her closest points to us, some sixteen to nineteen million miles away. Not very far, in terms of astronomical measurement, but to Dan and me very far indeed.

Two of these passings came and went. We had hoped there might be some sign from Xenephrene; even something hostile would have seemed to us better than nothing. Dan and I often sat in the night, gazing at the great purple-white planet.

Mysterious world, imperturbably blazing up there! It held captive for Dan the woman he loved; for me, my sister and father. Held them captive—if indeed they were alive, which is the best we could hope—held them and gave no sign! Beautiful, mysterious world—and sinister! Gazing up at it, my fancy roamed.

What strange sights and sounds and beings were there! We had had but a slight hint through Zetta, no more. And then it had been snatched away.

It is not important now for me to recount what these months brought on Earth, the adjustment to new conditions, new climate, new night and day. Volumes of history describe it fully—the myriad shifting events over the world's great surface, the new nations, new mingling of races— everything new, it seemed. Everything but human nature, the old characteristics, love, hate, jealousy, friendship, greed —nothing on Earth has ever changed them, and nothing will.

We did not know why father, Hulda and Zetta had been abducted. But we felt sure that they had been captured by the invaders and with them returned to Xenephrene. Why the invaders came at all, and then so hastily withdrew, we could not guess.

In the days that followed, Dan and I were distracted. Vainly he and I sought, tried to work out, some way by which we might get to Xenephrene. Before that terrible winter when the Great Change began, much serious progress had been made. But no programs could go forward with transportation at its present standstill. Projects had been stalled. Only a skeleton crew remained to safeguard the areas. Scientists told Dan and me what we already knew, of course: that any such attempt as we planned—a flight—well, there was no possible way even to begin to handle it.

I was far older now in spirit than that winter thirty-five months before. The frustrations, calamities and confusion had taken their toll. We do not age in regular progression of time passed, but in spurts of stressed mental strain and physical suffering. I aged, for besides losing a sister and father, I lost the girl Zetta—the loss of what might have been, for me and for her.

Love born of a glance, now to stay with me always? It was not that. I was not so youthful that I could cherish such romantic illusions.

But this I knew: something, that afternoon when she and

61

I first joined glances, sprang into being. As though over the gap from one world to another, from a man to a woman and back again, it sprang and clung reluctant to be broken. And it left its mark upon my mind and spirit. It was not to be: I believed that fully. But the consciousness was within me that it would have been a thing very beautiful.

And I was more mature, and, I think, a better man, just for the memory.

Thirty-five months! A dreary, hopeless interval to Dan and me. Dreary, for in the midst of all the world's turmoil we seemed to stand apart. Not actors, spectators merely, with our minds and spirits up there where the great purple star was shining. Thirty-five hopeless months, for it seemed that what we had lost was gone forever.

On February 4, 1970, Dan and I were living in Puerto Rico. Freddie was in Miami. Father's post in southern Chile was taken by one of his fellow scientists.

The world rolls on! Father was lost, his post filled and himself almost forgotten. How fatuously we mortals attach importance to ourselves! We strut our little hour upon the stage, some in the spotlight, some shrinking in the shadows by the backdrop. We miss our cues, fumble, and are abashed or terrified. But in a brief moment, no one cares. The curtain rings down, then up again, with the old play but new scenes and other actors; and the changing audience forgets we ever were on the stage at all.

Father's post was filled. Freddie and I had been down there in Chile one summer, but we did not like it and we came back. Summer! The very word had lost its meaning. They were begining now to call it the Day.

We came back in June, chasing the daylight, and located in Puerto Rico. Dan and his father were engaging in the new agriculture. The daylight and twilight months in the West Indies were found favorable for the raising of vegetables. Everyone was groping. What could or could not be done was as yet uncertain; but it promised to be a profitable business. Food of any kind, anywhere in the world, at any time, found a ready market. All the world governments were engaged in its purchase, its storage, and its distribution.

A new era was beginning; and in it some saw a more rational order than in the old. I am no economist. Yet now I could see quite clearly the fallacy of much that the world had thought the best. Tariff walls between the nations were gone now. The world in its necessity became one big family, working to maintain itself as best it could.

In the daylight in Puerto Rico, we were raising the vegetables to feed the people who were living in the darkness and cold of the south. Six months later, they would be doing the same for us.

It is not my purpose to indulge in economic theories here, though Dan and I often discussed them. Freddie was not interested. We wanted him with us. But though he came to Puerto Rico, he stayed in San Juan, often going up to Miami. The National Capital was still there, and the government had become seriously interested in Freddie's invention.

The world catastrophe had brought a great stimulus to scientific invention. New devices, born of the necessity of totally new world conditions, were being developed. It all took time. But every government was ready to help with funds. Freddie had perfected his motor financed by private enterprise, under government supervision.

More important than that, however, they were interested in producing his heat-ray projector in more powerful form. His new projector, he told us, was very nearly ready. Not for war purposes, of course. With characteristic thoughtlessness, the world had already almost forgotten the brief invasion from Xenephrene. Such a thing as that naturally never could happen again. And after what the world had been through, and was still enduring, war between our races was unthinkable.

Freddie's heat-ray, he said, would be used in the six months' Night against the cold. It had a myriad uses. With it, a ship might blaze a path down a frozen river. Water power might be utilized further into the long Night. Why, a city might even be sprayed with its beams and be kept spring-like despite the cold! Visions! But by such visions science moves ahead into the realism of achievement.

That long Night of '69 and '70, Dan and I spent housed

in, with the comparative comfort of our newly rebuilt and heated plantation house. Throughout January and February it snowed heavily: the tumbled little mountains of Puerto Rico were solid white.

Sometimes the leaden sky would clear. The stars and moon would glitter on the snow, so bright one could almost read outdoors. Our winter moon was magnificent. The moon's orbit about the earth was very little changed from before; its plane had shifted with us, scientists said, and the moon was pursuing very nearly its old path relative to us.

Dan and I had a small Arctic A flyer, and sleighs. We did not use the plane much. The indolence of the long night of enforced idleness was upon us. Most of the world was learning how to work hard in the daylight months, and to do nothing, gracefully, through the months of darkness. We read our books, studied, planned and talked.

It would have been very pleasant, had there not been that constant sense of what we had lost. Father, Hulda—and Zetta. I had spoken very little of Zetta to Dan. The dreams of what might have been were my own. Even with him, I could not share them.

And then came February 4, 1970. The long night was fully upon us, the twilight days were passed—midwinter was in early April. Dan and I had been out after breakfast for a drive in the sleigh. We had returned for luncheon with Dan's parents. I was on the veranda, enveloped in furs, pacing up and down in the snow. Dan, with his cigar, came out and joined me.

There is sometimes a very queer directness to the fate which governs our lives—and a great unexpectedness. We walk in the dark, with an open road or a chasm yawning before us, all unaware of which it might be. Or we may be standing at the threshold of a shining garden of hope and happiness, walking in the dark toward its gate, with heavy heart because we do not see that it is there.

Dan and I were like that now. January, 1970, had been the second time that Xenephrene passed at its closest point to earth. We had hoped that something might happen to give us news of father. But nothing did.

Gradually our hope had been dying. The January days dragged through their brief twilights into the solid winter night. We gave up hope.

Xenephrene was drawing ahead of the Earth again, with millions of miles of lengthening distance between the worlds. No sign from the great purple planet; and we both felt that now all hope of hearing from father was gone.

Thoughts like these possessed me as I paced the veranda that afternoon. They were in Dan's mind too, I am sure. But when he joined me, neither of us spoke of them.

It was clear and cold. The snow on the veranda crunched and creaked under our tread. Beyond the incongruous coconut railing the knoll-tops showed white, with a blue-white beam of light slanting out from one of the side windows. There was no moon, only a deep purple sky, with the sharply glittering silver stars. To the south, below the horizon, we knew that the sun at this hour was hovering. But it was too far down even to pale the stars now. Xenephrene was down there near it, invisible to us of the north. Dan and I paced in silence, or talked idly of the now commonplace things of the new era of the world.

"They claim they can keep the falls of the Iguazu open all year," said Dan. "And send the power even as far up as here."

There had been most disastrous floods throughout the world when, with the coming daylight, the snow and ice had melted. Watercourses were unable to handle the sudden, abnormal flow. But new channels were forming: nature and man alike were making adjustments to the new conditions.

"If they could only send us heat from the south," said Dan. "I mean direct, natural heat. These new transformers of the power waves may be all right, but—"

"Freddie's invention can . . . I don't mean send it, but produce it—"

"Some day," said Dan, "we'll be able to spray all our land here with that contrivance of his. Hah! That would be a great idea, wouldn't it?" He chuckled with an ironical gibe at the absent Freddie. But still he was more than half serious.

65

"Imagine us, Peter, getting out in the June twilight, helping the snow to melt by spraying it with heat—warming up the frozen soil, getting it plowed and planted a month earlier. If we could get our perishable vegetables down to the Argentine ahead of the others, they'd bring mighty big prices. I was reading what might be done with tomatoes—"

He checked himself abruptly, gripped my arm with a force that whirled me around. We stood at the veranda rail.

"Good lord, Peter, look at that!"

From overhead near the zenith, a shooting star came blazing down. I had never seen one so brilliant. A great yellow-red ball of fire, with a tail of flame. It seemed to take long seconds as it soundlessly fell across the sky before us—down with a blaze to the northern horizon where the Caribbean lay, a dim, dark purple in the starlight.

We breathed again. "That didn't burn itself out," said Dan. "I'll wager that was a meteorite—actually landed somewhere. . . ."

"Northwest," I said. "Florida way. It certainly seemed close to us, didn't it?"

We went back to our pacing. There was nothing particularly unusual in seeing a meteor fall across the sky. But we were both silent, wondering. We had caught just a glimpse of the gateway to our renewed hope. We did not know it then, but we both sensed it.

An hour passed. From within the house, old man Cain called, "Oh, Dan—come here, listen to this."

The radio announcer was relaying an item from Curaçao. In the twilight at Williamstadt they had seen what seemed to be a meteorite fall into the sea near the Venezuelan coast.

"Another!" exclaimed Dan.

An hour later, still another meteorite was reported. It had fallen somewhere in the region of Victoria Nyanza—in the lake, perhaps, or along its shores.

In the silence I could hear the tiny sound of Freddie's voice. We had switched on the two-way circuit.

"Dan? Dan Cain?"

"Yes. That you, Freddie?"

"Yes. Listen—I'm in Miami. A meteorite fell in the Okeechobee region. They've got it, and it's cracked open. Was pretty well burned—but a big one. Hollow inside. They cracked into it—they found— Oh, Dan, they phoned me from Moorehaven just a few minutes ago. They—" Freddie's voice broke with his excitement.

"They—what, Freddie? Take it easy—can't understand you."

"I'm coming, Dan. By plane—I'll get away about eight o'clock. Peter there? Good! See you about midnight—soon as they bring it here to me, I'll bring it to you."

"Bring what? *What*, Freddie?"

"The cylinder. Whatever it is—I haven't seen it. They're bringing it—they've got it. Heat-proof, insulated metal cylinder—they say it's engraved 'Peter Vanderstuyft, Puerto Rico —Rush.' I'm bringing it, Dan. Tell Peter. It's a message from Xenephrene! It must be! A message from Peter's father!"

VIII

FROM ACROSS THE VOID

WE HELPED Freddie unload the cylinder from his plane. He arrived about midnight, flying alone with his precious burden. It was a cylindrical metal container, some ten feet long by three feet in diameter—a strange looking, purple-brown metal, smooth and shining like burnished copper. White metal handles were on the cylinder—and down one of its bulging sides was crudely engraved the inscription, "Peter Vanderstuyft, Puerto Rico—Rush."

The thing weighed perhaps two hundred pounds. It was warm, yet clammy to the touch, as though sweating. And though it appeared smooth, under my fingertips I could feel that it was pitted and scarred—blistered as though by tremendous heat.

We labored up the hill with it, and deposited it on the floor in the Cains' living room, gathering over it, wondering how it might be opened.

The message from Xenephrene! It had come at last; and strangely enough, I did not feel that this was remarkable. We had been waiting for it. And here it was at our feet, oddly fashioned—mute, but waiting passively to give up its secret.

We were all trembling. Freddie had discarded his furs and helmet, but his hands were stiff with the cold.

"How do we get into it? They didn't want to open it—I didn't try either."

Dan was on the floor beside the cylinder, running his hands over its surface. His father and mother crowded upon him. Old man Cain's jaw was dropped with his awe. Mrs. Cain chattered, "Heavens, what next! Dan, what is it? Is it from Professor Vanderstuyft? Is he all right? And dear little Hulda? She's all right, isn't she, Dan? That's what this means, doesn't it?"

Dan jumped to his feet. "Yes, Mother, that's what we hope it means." He kissed her, then pushed her away, gently but very firmly. "You go to bed, Mother. Father, you go too. We'll be working here some hours—in the morning we'll tell you all about it. We'll know by then."

Freddie, Dan and I were left alone. The double doors and double windows were closed against the cold. A broad coal fire burned in the grate. The room was warm and silent, and blue with the light-tube, which cast its beam down upon the cylinder. Freddie said, with a hush in his voice, "We'd have been afraid to try and open it anyway, in Miami. . . . You don't suppose it would explode if we pound at it, do you?"

The sweating thing was strangely sinister, despite its friendly inscription. Dan was again bending over it. Freddie added:

"It was in a meteorite—some strange rock, or metal. Evidently not natural. It was burned, fused and shapeless by the heat of its fall through our atmosphere. You can see where the heat has burned into the cylinder—"

68

"Wait!" said Dan abruptly. "Listen!"

With our ears close to the metal a tiny hum was audible. The thing was humming inside. Alive! Vibrant! Humming with that strange, almost gruesome whine which brought to my memory the crimson sound of Xenephrene invaders when Robinson and Davis had attacked them.

It was half an hour before, with the utmost caution, we got the cylinder open. On one of its sides we found four slightly raised circles and four small depressions, numbered from one to eight. And the words, crudely scratched on the metal, "Peter, press one, three, five and eight."

A lid came off. We wouldn't have seen the cracks where it had fitted. It stuck, fused by heat. But we carefully forced it, and at length it came away.

The human mind is subject to queer vagaries. There was just an instant, as we lifted the metal panel, when there flashed to me the vague horror that this was a coffin: that we were about to behold a corpse—wrapped and sent to us like a mummy. Hulda! Zetta! A ghastly gibe, sent to mock us from this sinister unknown world!

Then the instant of unreasoning panic passed, though cold sweat still stood in beads on my forehead from those fleeting, horrible fancies.

The interior of the cylinder was divided into orderly compartments. Metal boxes; cones; cubes of metal; diaphragms; coils of white wire—packed, wrapped and lashed in orderly array, each piece seemingly set in springs to absorb the landing shock. A white lining was inside the cylinder, smooth as mica—insulation against the heat, perhaps. A strange, vague odor arose; and we could hear the humming now more plainly. It seemed to come from several metal globes the size of a man's head. Dead black metal; four or five of them were packed near the center of the cylinder. Around them a dim radiance was hovering.

"Wait!" admonished Dan. "Take it easy!" Freddie, in his excitement, would have begun rummaging. "Wait! There must be some instructions somewhere. Don't touch anything until you know what you're doing."

We found the box of instructions. It was, indeed, the

most prominent thing before us, though we had overlooked it—a flat metal case some twelve inches square and half as thick, packed edgewise. Clipped to its top was a white roll of what seemed to be paper.

Dan gingerly removed it and unrolled it—a translucent white animal skin, possibly. And with writing on it! At last the doubts and fears that were within us were dispelled: the writing was in father's firm, smooth unhurried script.

"To my son, Peter Vanderstuyft. In Puerto Rico care of Ezra John Cain, or the Amalgamated Broadcasters Association, United States of America. Please forward at once."

And then the words: "Peter, detailed instructions inside. We are safe—your father, Hulda and Zetta."

Zetta! The gates to the shining garden were swung wide for me then!

We sat around the table under the blue light tube with father's communication, which we found inside the flat metal case, spread before us. It was a voluminous manuscript, nearly a hundred handwritten pages. Part of it was an all too brief letter; then there were passages of instructions, scientific data, notes and diagrams. We glanced at them hurriedly, and in a voice which in spite of me I could not hold steady, I read the letter aloud to Dan and Freddie.

Under Gardens, Xenephrene
Earth-date January, 1970

Peter, I trust and pray that this, or one of its duplicates which I am dispatching, may reach you. I am launching five cylinders. Any one of them will answer the purpose, but if you can possess yourself of more than one, so much the better. I suggest, before you read further, that you guard against taking any stranger into the confidence of this communication. I want Smith and Dan Cain with you when you read this. I know that I can depend upon them both, as I can upon you, my son.

I glanced up from the page to the solemn, intent faces

of Freddie and Dan. Neither spoke. Freddie's face was flushed with excitement. His breath came fast between parted lips. But Dan was pale and grim. His lean brown fingers gripped the table edge with whitened knuckles, and there was a brief silence.

"Go on," said Dan tensely.

I went back to the page. "He wants utmost secrecy." Unconsciously I lowered my voice. Freddie swung to the radio table to verify that the lever of the outgoing audiophone was off.

I went on reading:

If this should fall into other hands than those of my son, I beg that you who read it will read no further than this paragraph. Or, if you do, that loyalty to your nation—to your world—will bid you hold it secret. And if you value your own welfare—the very lives of those most dear to you—at once you will deliver this cylinder and its contents intact to the government of the United States of America, with instructions that my son, Peter Vanderstuyft of the Amalgamated Broadcasters Association, be located and the cylinder delivered to him. Or to Frederick Smith, Royal Dutch Astronomical Bureau, Anco, Chile; or to Daniel J. Cain, Factor, Puerto Rico.

Peter, there is much I would tell you—but I have no time now. We are safe. Hulda and Zetta are with me, and well. I have been ill but am better now. The things, Peter, that I have seen and done! To name them, even if I could find the words, would be to no purpose. I am trying to communicate with you—and Dan and Frederick—to allay your immediate fears for our safety. But more than that, Peter! The threat against our Earth, as we saw it thirty-four months ago, is far greater now! For that, I would caution you, or anyone loyal to Earth who may read this, of the necessity for secrecy.

Enemies of Earth—of a character, of a plane of being, oh, Peter, you could not guess—may be on Earth now. I do not know. I fear they are. Some may have made the trip at the conjunction seventeen months ago. We suspect they did. Or if not, we fear some may be embarking from here now.

Guard yourself from them with secrecy of your actions and a constant watchfulness. I can suggest no other ways. If I could come to you—if I could bring Hulda back to you—I would make the trip instead of sending this message. But we cannot, or at least I think it would not be advisable.

I am needed here. Needed by this world—by all those in it who stand for right and justice and adherence to the laws of the Almighty God Who rules all of us of every world. And I think also that the welfare of our beloved world can best be safeguarded by my remaining here for the present.

I will come to the point, Peter. There is so much for me to set down beyond a mere letter to you with explanations which well may wait until later. I want you here, Peter! And, if they think it advisable to trust their lives to such an adventure—I want Dan and Frederick to come with you. Will you come!

I ask you as though I were inviting you across one of our little oceans at home! Yet I—so much more fully than yourselves—realize what this is that I so casually ask! You are young, all three of you, and the spirit of adventure and recklessness runs high in healthy youth. I am playing upon it. I need not ask. I know you will come, if—as I pray may be the case —I have now provided you with the means—

My hand holding his written page was shaking. Freddie burst out, with a return of his old boyish enthusiasm, "I should say we *would* come! What a question!"

I heard Dan murmur, "At last!"

Within me was a surge of emotion, a thrill of exaltation, mingled perhaps with a thrill of fear at the unknown crowding now so close upon me. And the thought of Zetta,

72

mentioned so briefly in those written words from across the void! Yet from every line her name leaped at me, sang soundlessly in my head.

The image of her was never more clear in my memory. Here in this very room where we had clasped hands and stood and swayed and wondered what Nature might be doing to us who, an instant before, had been strangers— an image of her seemed here now hovering in the shadows of the room behind the tense, bent figure of Dan. It was so clear that I almost felt that something of her must have come with this letter: some unspoken longing of hers which she had sent to me as, perhaps in silence, she had watched father writing.

I think there *was* something. I felt it; and within me, my spirit was murmuring a welcome and an answer.

"Go on," said Dan gruffly. "Read it, Peter."

I shuffled the papers. "There isn't much more. He's evidently—"

"He's sent us the materials—the mechanisms out of which to build a vehicle," exclaimed Freddie. "It's evident that—"

Dan murmured, "Too late this time! Seventeen months— seventeen more months to wait—"

I laughed. An intoxication was upon me at the thought of it. "Wait, nothing! We'll be busy, don't worry about that! Time is relative. With the inspiration—if we can do it— Freddie, what the devil?"

Freddie had leaped to his feet. He was standing with his head cocked, listening. There was no sound, save the vague humming from the opened cylinder stretched on the floor at our feet.

"Thought I heard something."

"You didn't," I said.

"Where?" demanded Dan. "The audiophone? It's off— completely dead."

"Outside?" I suggested. I half rose from my seat.

Freddie looked puzzled. He went to the door, listened, and returned. He asked, "You don't hear anything?"

"No," I said. "Where?"

"I don't know. Here—I mean here, right here with us. I—I guess I imagined it."

"I guess you did," said Dan. But his gaze swept the room with a tense expectancy.

My heart was pounding. We all three drew nearer together, as though for instinctive protection against something we could almost but not quite hear.

"We're nervous," said Dan. "Imagining things. It's that damned weird humming. Go on, Peter."

I resumed the letter:

You will find in this cylinder the vital element necessary to the conquering of gravity. Reet, which a bountiful nature supplies here, is a very wonderful thing, Peter. With it, and with such materials available on Earth, which my notes herewith describe fully, I believe you will have no great difficulty in constructing your vehicle. I have sent you the basic mechanisms already assembled in each of their integral parts—

Freddie again interrupted me. "Where's that draft coming from? It's cold. You got some window open, Dan?"

I was conscious of cold air in the room. The door to the adjoining bedroom—the room father had once occupied, but which now was unused—stood half open. The draft of chill air seemed to be coming from there. And then we all three heard a bump in there. It brought us all to our feet!

"Shutter banging," said Dan. "Mother must have left the window partly open—shutter banging, there's a wind starting."

"We should have checked that room," Peter muttered.

We followed Dan with a precipitous haste. It was in semi-darkness. The window was partly raised from the bottom. Cold air was sweeping in. But the shutter was fastened tightly back against the outside wall: it could not bang. Dan closed the window. None of us made any comment. Back at the living room table I began the letter again:

There is very little I need say further, Peter. My

74

notes, diagrams and instructions explain fully. Attached
to several of the mechanisms, you will find individual
instruction sheets.

You will need funds. No doubt, Peter, by now you
will have been able to possess yourself legally of my
money, as the law has eased to such an extent due
to world conditions. Use what you have and can
obtain freely, Peter. Take from Dan as little as possible—

The light over my head suddenly dimmed to half its
volume. Freddie gave a startled exclamation. Dan cursed.

"Something seems determined to interrupt us," I said. I
held the letter up to the light. "I can read it."

"What the—" Freddie began.

"Two o'clock," said Dan. "They only give us half strength
ight after 2 A.M. New ruling in Puerto Rico for the Night
months."

Freddie sank back. I read:

Do your best. You ought to be able to start at the
next conjunction. Your start, your navigation—all of
this you will find in my instruction sheets. Before you
arrive here, open the special sealed envelope marked
"Landing Instructions." Follow them implicitly.

I will meet you. I have had fairly good conditions
for scientific work here, Peter. You will find my instructions accurate, all my data fully explicit. With
Frederick's scientific knowledge, you should have no
trouble. Hulda sends love. She says, love to Dan,
especially. Good old Dan! We feel very close to you
all in spirit, Peter—in spite, or perhaps even because
of the void between us. You will cross it—oh, my son,
be very careful! Follow every detail of my instructions. We will be waiting, impatiently. Zetta is here,
watching me as I write. Strange, dear little Zetta.
So remarkable a friend—

A cry from Dan interrupted me. I had been standing
wkwardly holding the letter up to the light. The room
'as dim, with shadows crowding close upon us. At our

75

feet the opened cylinder lay under the half-strength blue light. It was partly in shadow. At Dan's startled cry I looked down. A red radiance hovered across the cylinder in the gloom there! A faint glow of crimson! And there sounded a low gutteral whine. The crimson sound! In the room here with us!

Dan leaped. From within the cylinder one of its metal boxes was coming out! It came up with a jerk, as though raised by some invisible hand. A small, dead-white metal cube. Enveloped in a vague red glow, it came up to the level of my waist and moved away through the air.

Dan went leaping over the cylinder. He struck something solid, and fell prone on the floor with the metal cube clattering beside him.

There was a confusion of sounds, a sudden unearthly scream. Then Dan's voice shouting, "I've got it, Freddie. Oh Peter—"

Dan was struggling on the floor with something. I could see his arms encircling it. Something large. He rolled, fought. Freddie jumped for him. I dropped the letter, dashed to where both Freddie and Dan were rolling on the floor, gripping something in a glow of humming red sound.

They both shouted, "Peter, watch out! Keep away! Watch him—grab him if he slips loose—"

I was standing over them. From the red confusion a naked arm emerged for an instant. I seized it—a queerly light but solid arm of bone and flesh and muscle. But it jerked away. There was a crash as the table overturned.

"Peter! Hold him! Peter—Freddie, let go of me—don't be a fool! Let go of me, I tell you!"

Something caught me in the face with a burning blow like a firebrand. I staggered back; my flailing arms hit nothing. The room was whining with sound. On the floor Dan and Freddie in a fog of red glow, now dissipating, were shouting and struggling to disentangle themselves from each other.

I heard a thump: the sound of running, padding footsteps. Before I could recover my balance from the blow in the face, the sound was gone. A clatter in the adjoining room. Then silence.

Dan and Freddie stood erect, panting, shaking and confused. In the bedroom, the window was open again. The intruder had gone. On the floor by the cylinder lay the white metal cube which had so nearly been stolen from us. We lifted it up. It seemed uninjured. On it was a tag, with father's inscription: "Reet catalyst concentrated—B Formula. Guard this well, Peter! Without it, your enterprise would be impossible!"

IX

PIONEERS INTO SPACE

June 14, 1971. I set down the date with my recollection that it was for me the most momentous day of my life up to that time. And I think, for Dan and Freddie also—the day upon which, after more than sixteen months of activity, we three were ready at last for the trip to Xenephrene. The events of those sixteen months were to me the mere bridging of an interval unimportant save in its consummation.

We were constantly harassed because of the lethargy and lack of interest which the government showed in our project, until very recently. No alarm we could sound appeared to make an impression. It's strange how governments, throughout history, have buried their heads in the sands—reacting, very probably, to the dictates of their constituents —acting, or actually being, oblivious to the possible peril coming closer each day. Blindly going forward, ignoring its possibility! Here we were—and I feel it would have been different had father, with his influence, been here to do the prodding—but here we were, with all our great ambitions and accomplishments in space travel, so few months ago, our ingenious scientific weapons and defences—

Yet now, even after the warning from Xenephrene, we were

77

still fighting only for existence, for trade, for agricultural superiority!

And lying dormant, disfigured by the elements and unmanned, were the tombstones of our neglect: launching pads, missiles, weapons innumerable and varied, many still in the experimental stage. What had become of our initiative, our foresight? How had we, an intelligent people such as we were considered to be, permitted this great arsenal of protection and adventure to sink into disntegration and complete disuse?

Ironically, perhaps, it was the unchanging human weakness: the urge was not to spend money, but to acquire it!

There were times when all thought we would fail with our project. I am not of a scientific trend of mind; nor is Dan. Both he and I depended upon Freddie for a complete understanding of father's data.

Even so, it seemed to Dan and to me in our impatience and futility with our own lack of knowledge, lack of scientific training, that there was a great deal about father's instructions that Freddie himself but half understood. Had we not had several of the nation's leading scientists behind us, I doubt we could have accomplished our final result.

The whole enterprise was conducted quietly with a minimum of people having any knowledge of it whatever; and though distorted rumors crept out, the actual facts were carefully concealed.

During most of this period—these seemingly interminable months—Dan, Freddie and I were in Miami where, in a vault loaned us by the government, the scientists worked with Freddie. Here our mechanisms were assembled; a thousand abstruse chemical and physical problems were solved.

The work progressed steadily, though with occasional maddening holdups. Father had suggested that the outer shell be constructed of alexite, that strange alloy, largely aluminum, after the process perfected by the Russ, Alexia. World conditions made it difficult for some of the material to be quickly obtained. But they were obtained, which showed what could be done where there was determination, and the shell was cast almost on the date set for it in Freddie's schedule.

The daylight months of 1970, in Miami, brought heat almost intolerable. Weird change from what always before had been the normal! The spring twilight thaws; the brief periods of lengthening days until soon the day and night were equal; then, each twenty-four hours, a longer day, a lesser night. Swiftly changing, until soon the sun never set. Blistering summer. Then again the sun touched the horizon . . . rose . . . in twenty-four hours dipped a trifle. Night a minute long! Queer cycle! But we had grown used to it, for human life springs swiftly to adjust itself to environment.

The summer of 1970 dragged itself past. In January, 1971, with the fall twilight days passing and night again upon us, the vehicle shell was cast. Assembling of the mechanism began in February. By April, in the frigid darkness of midwinter, I think we could have been ready to start. But Xenephrene was too far away. Daily now she was overtaking the Earth.

We had to await the June conjunction when at her closest point for the year, father's data told us the intervening distance would be some seventeen and a half million miles. His notes named twelve o'clock noon, June 14, as our best starting time. And in this, as in every other detail, we were determined to follow his instructions to the letter.

We had been worried all these months over father's warning concerning the presence on Earth of enemies from Xenephrene. Indeed, that first evening in the Cain plantation house, when the storage battery of the Reet Catalyst had so nearly been stolen from us, had proven that father's fears were fully justified. But the precious white metal cube was unharmed; and there was nothing else missing from the cylinder, as we had at first feared.

The intruder had left no trace of himself. But he was a man, undoubtedly human like ourselves. Dan and Freddie had grappled with him. I had felt his burning blow upon my face. There was a red blistered welt there for many days. Dan and Freddie were burned about the hands and face.

Curious marks! I say burned, for perhaps that best describes it. But it was not that. A queer irritation of the skin and flesh where they had been exposed to contact with the crimson radiance. It left within a week; and the ringing in our ears, which for a day we all feared might presage deafness, was gone in a like period. Our eyes too, were left smarting and burning. For a day afterward I found my sight queerly blurring at intervals; and any sudden light blinded me momentarily, as one is blinded who steps abruptly from darkness into light. But all these unpleasant sensations passed.

This crimson radiance had been undoubtedly of a very weak intensity. It had not been used as a weapon, but merely as a cloak of invisibility, behind which the intruder had evidently felt he could steal the cylinder and escape. This we realized, though of the nature of the radiance we knew not much more than before. Nor was there anything in father's data to enlighten us.

We feared a repetition of this encounter. But in this vault we had maximum security. It was incredible, of course, that upon Earth there would be one man from Xenephrene, and no more. We learned afterward that there were many, but at this time no trace of them was found.

It was June 4 when at last our vehicle was completely ready—save its provisioning, some Earth scientific apparatus which father had bade us bring, and personal effects. The assembling was complete, the navigating mechanism installed, tested and in working order.

It was then, and not until then, that success seemed assured. And with the relief of it, we all realized what a strain we had been under. By comparison, what lay ahead seemed simple. But that fancy passed; and though we never said so, apprehension soon descended upon us again.

For myself a thousand doubts assailed me. Could Freddie successfully navigate us in this strange vehicle from one world to another? He had done no space travel before.

Could he, by mathematical formulae which to me seemed incredibly abstruse, and mechanisms in our vehicle which even he only half understood, accomplish this feat? Alone, unaided, a pilot heading into trackless space, with only father's complicated notes to guide him?

Freddie, during these last days, was pale and silent. Not for anything would Dan or I have voiced our fears. But Freddie was aware of them, for they matched his own. Thin-lipped and solemn he sat for hours each day within the vehicle; and sometimes he would slip away from Dan and me during the hours of sleep, and we would find him there, poring over father's data, or working at seemingly endless calculations.

Spring twilight was mounting during the first two weeks of June. The spring thaws were at hand. On June 13 we made our final inspection of the vehicle to be sure its equipment was complete. It was a small affair—as small as the one in which Zetta had arrived. And similar in shape: a flattened globe twenty-one feet in vertical diameter and thirty feet across its middle width.

The thin shell of alexite gave it a dull gleaming white color. The exterior was reinforced with a thick rolled belt of alexite like an equator around the globe's bulging middle.

There were two vertical reinforcing circular bands: passing through its poles they divided its surface into four equal segments. Into each of these segments two small bullseye windows were set, one directly above the other. And in one segment, near the bottom, was a small, narrow door. The top and bottom of the globe were flattened to a level area some six feet square, as though a section had been neatly sliced off, to form a small lower floor and a small roof. Each was set with a bullseye glass windowpane.

Such was the exterior aspect of our vehicle. I chanced to stand alone for a moment a few hours before our start, regarding it as it lay in the small vault which had been built to house it. A tiny little world! Little white globe, so soon to be whirling through space with its three human inhabitants! And I was to be one of the three!

The globe's interior was reinforced with a lining of alexite ribs, and a brittle wire mesh cast into the alexite shell. It was tested for pressure: in the vacuum of space the outward pressure of our air content would have exploded a shell less perfectly built. Father had calculated all this. His calculations proved correct. We had a wide margin of safety.

The globe inside was divided by two horizontal floorings into three compartments. The lowest one, to which the narrow doorway gave entrance, had a floor six feet square, bulging concave walls, and a ceiling some seven feet above the floor.

The compartment was our instrument room, and observatory. It had four side windows, and the lower window which comprised our floor. Between the side windows, the instruments were fitted in racks. The control table was here, and a portion of the navigating mechanism.

The middle story—much the largest of the three—contained our sleeping cots, our meager cooking arrangements, our food stock, and most of the mechanical apparatus for the navigating of the globe.

The upper compartment, in size and shape like the lower, held our personal effects, our water supply, heating instruments, and the Regnalt-Dillon air purifier, with the pumps, fans and distributors. In flight, this would always remain the upper segment of the vehicle. We would turn over after leaving the Earth and fall toward Xenephrene.

The last day came: June 14, with its raw, thawing chill in the air, and a twilight at noon which almost promised a sunrise. Dan and I had not slept for twenty-four hours, in the fever of our excitement. Nor had Freddie. He had not left the vehicle, just sat there in the lower compartment with the control buttons on his small table and a sheaf of father's instructions, studying them over and over. Once, when I bade him sleep, he turned upon me so sharply that I retreated in haste. I brought him a cup of coffee.

"Here, Freddie." I held it out, a peace offering. He glanced up with his pale face and tired eyes.

"Oh, thanks, Peter—very much."

An emotion swept me—between man and woman comes

the most strongly tempestuous human emotion, but there can be between a man and his friend an emotion wholly dissimilar, but of equally powerful bond. I felt it then as I laid my hand upon Freddie's shoulder.

"Thanks," he repeated. "Sorry I snapped at you, Peter."

Men are most inarticulate with each other when deeply stirred. I nodded.

Three hours later we left the Earth. There was a pathos to our leaving, mingled with the excitement of it. Any unusual adventure in life seems to bring into play the whole gamut of human emotions.

There stood Dan's old father and mother! Not for them did Xenephrene hold any lure! They were giving their only son to what must have seemed a mad tempting of fate. They had said little.

What passed between them and Dan, I never knew. But they came to the vault exit to see us off. They stood in a far corner of the room, apart from the scientists and few officials who were there to speed us.

A brief, strangely dramatic scene, our leaving!

We stood there at the small doorway of our tiny world. Attendants rolled back the roof of the vault; the stars gleamed down upon us. The room was dim; it seemed full of vague, moving shadows—people to whom I must say goodby now and leave, perhaps forever.

Someone called out, "Eleven fifty-four! Better get inside, Smith."

Freddie glanced at his watch. "Yes. Well . . . goodby. Goodby, everybody—wish us luck." His tone was queerly stilted.

Then men's hands were shaking mine. Men were clapping me on the back. And then I found myself with Dan before his parents. Trembling old man and woman; a pity for them swept me.

"Goodby, Peter."

"Goodby," I said. Mrs. Cain kissed me. I added, "We'll be back soon. Goodby."

Freddie's voice was calling, "Hurry up, there!" I turned away. But Dan lingered. From the doorway I had a glimpse

83

of him as with his big arms he caught his mother up to kiss her goodby, while his father clung to him.

Then Dan was with us. The small heavy door swung closed and locked upon us.

Eleven fifty-nine! Freddie sat at his table, his fingers on the row of buttons. In the gloom, the only light was a glow upon the chronometer face with its second-hand making the last circle. Noon! There was a vague hum as the Reet current went on. The floor beneath my feet stirred slightly, then steadied. Through the window I caught a glimpse of the room outside, its vaulted sides slipping silently downward.

We had started!

Had our voyage been an adventure unique in modern history, I should be restrained to describe it here in detail. But since these few stirring years I am describing, interplanetary voyaging has become a common thing. But an account of Xenephrene? That's a different matter. I doubt if any world will ever be found comparable to Xenephrene.

As everyone knows now, Mars is nothing like it; nor Venus; nor Mercury. They talk already of going to Jupiter, to Uranus, to Neptune. It is possible, of course. And in a few lifetimes beyond my own, they will be striving to reach the distant stars, for the spirit of adventure in man is insatiable.

Our voyage was unmarked by any untoward incident. Our sensations at first, the novelty of it, stirred us all as we had never been stirred before. The first plunge into the dead blackness of space, with the stars and the sun and all the worlds blazing like torches, is an experience never to be forgotten.

The first look backward upon a dull-red crescent Earth!

The man or woman who has had that look will feel ever afterward a humbleness of spirit, a sense of our own infinite unimportance in the great plan of the universe. It is only the man who revolves his mind in its own humdrum little rut who thinks that he and what he stands for is the sum-total of real importance and goodness in the universe! What differs from himself, from his own standards of thought and living, he thinks must of necessity be inferior.

84

The traveler knows it is not so. Distant places, distant worlds, distant people—are different. Not necessarily inferior. Other races have different standards, different modes of thought from our own. Not better, perhaps; nor worse. Just different.

One of our poets once wrote: "Though patriotism flatter, still shall wisdom find an equal portion dealt to all mankind." The traveler knows that is true.

I come to the time now when in our tiny voyaging world we found ourselves, according to Freddie's calculations, at a distance of no more than two hundred and fifty thousand miles from Xenephrene. As close as our own moon is to the Earth.

Our vehicle had turned over soon after starting. The Earth lay in the star-field above us, a glittering red-white point, not very different from a million others. Beneath us, seen from the lower window, we were falling toward Xenephrene. It hung there amid the stars. To the naked eye now it was a tremendous, moon-like crescent, purple-red on its lighted area. The shadowed part of its circle could be faintly seen, a dull-red shadow.

We sat in the lower compartment—Freddie, as usual, by his table, with Dan and me beside him. Freddie was thoroughly rested now. At the start he had worn himself to the verge of exhaustion. But once we were well away from the Earth he found confidence in the verified correctness of his calculations.

We were upon our course. All was going well; and to our voyage, with the novelty dulling, came that monotony which is the chief characteristic of space-travel. There was little to do, save sleep, prepare our meals, and keep watch at our instruments to see that no asteroid or meteor crossed our path with dangerous nearness. Freddie's calculations were from then on his only labor. Dan and I did the rest.

We sat now with Freddie, who had called to us. The quarter of a million mile point from Xenephrene was an objective to which all three of us had looked forward with keenest interest.

"We're there," called Freddie. We came down to find him

with sparkling eyes and flushed face. "Two-fifty thousand, eight hundred odd miles." He shoved his papers away from him. "I brought us, didn't I? I did it!"

We clapped him on the back. We all felt as though the Rubicon were crossed.

"Now," said Freddie, "we can open Professor Vanderstuyft's last instruction sheet."

Father had sent us in the cylinder one bulky envelope which expressly he had stated was not to be opened until we were within two hundred and fifty thousand miles of our destination.

He called it "Landing Instructions". He had mentioned it several times in a way almost ominously mysterious. Everything concerning Xenephrene itself father had omitted from his other notes, as though not to confuse our minds with details not then necessary. But now, we felt, as we neared the other world, the mystery that clung to it would have to be unfolded.

The prospect made our hearts pound, for there clung always to our thoughts of this other world a sense of the uncanny—we were plunging, very soon now, into something weird, perhaps gruesome. But I thought of little Zetta and I knew that though it would be a strange world, weird and bizarre, it could not be gruesome.

Freddie was holding father's envelope. "Here it is—we can open it now. It's addressed to you, Peter—you read it to us."

I took the envelope and broke its seal with fingers that were trembling in spite of all my efforts to steady them.

X

LANDING TO FACE THE UNKNOWN

To ONE OF ominiscience who could have observed us three as we sat there, it must have been a very strange scene indeed.

The tiny white globe which was our world rotated slowly on its vertical axis, a mere white speck hanging in the black intensity of space. With its concave, encircling shell, that lower compartment, with the iron ladder leading above, the three of us sitting there at the table: Freddie alert, with keenly roving eyes, his hand out of habit resting idly beside the control buttons; Dan's great length sprawled in his low chair, his shirt open at the throat, a growth of blond stubble on his face, his hair tousled—he lounged in an attitude of ease, yet his tenseness was obvious; myself sitting upright, with father's papers in my trembling hands. Shadows surrounded us, only one small light casting its glow upon me; and through the window beneath our feet came the upflung glare of Xenephrene, like a tremendous crescent moon bathing us in its purple light.

The silence! There is no silence like that of space. Upon Earth we hear always a myriad tiny sounds and are largely unaware of them. Without them, in space, the silence seems to scream its emptiness.

Dan cleared his throat nervously. "Go ahead, Peter—what does it say?"

I rustled the papers. Father's script began with characteristic abruptness:

If you have done as I requested, you are now within a quarter of a million miles of this world. Comparatively so close to us—oh, my son, I do hope that you are there! Soon, then, I shall see you, have you with me. I am growing old, Peter. The ties of blood seem to strengthen as we grow older. It has been lonely without you, my son, even though I have had dear Hulda—and little Zetta, of whom we grow more fond every day.

But this is no time for sentiment. I assume that Frederick and Dan are with you. I must be brief. Succinct. There are several things which I now must make plain to you three. If there is anything here, Peter, which Dan and you do not understand, Frederick will make it clear.

87

The few astronomical facts concerning Xenephrene which now you should know, are these: It is a globe flattened at the poles, expanded at the equator—rather more so than the Earth. Polar diameter, sixty-five hundred miles. Equatorial diameter seventy-eight hundred miles. Thus it is only slightly smaller than our Earth. Its average density I believe is about that of the Earth. Its mass, hence, is but little less than Earth. Gravitation, about the same. You will notice, in this respect, hardly any difference.

Xenephrene's present orbit about our sun is an ellipse rather more eccentric than Earth's—more comparable to that of Mercury. I believe it is not yet stabilized. There may even be a tendency toward a breaking of the ellipse at its aphelion—I sometimes shudder at the thought, if we should all be here on Xenephrene. Frederick will understand—"

I glanced at Dan. "Well, if he does, we don't."
"Never mind," said Freddie. But he did not smile.
I read on:

Xenephrene rotates on its axis once in twenty-two · hours, thirty-seven minutes, ten seconds, as we measure time on Earth. This axis is not inclined to the plane of its orbit, but is almost exactly vertical. Hence we have here no change of seasons. And throughout the year, the periods of day and night alternate in exact and unchanging relative lengths.

Here in the country of the Garlands, we are situated at about eight degrees south latitude. Thus, near the equator, our days are always some eleven hours and nineteen minutes long; and our night but a few seconds shorter.

Xenephrene has one moon—Pyrena, we call it. You will already have seen it, even with your small telescope, no doubt. I will not go into the elements of its orbit now, or describe its phases as we nightly see them. A beautiful sight, Peter. It is really the sun for

Xenephrene—or at least it was, before Xenephrene came to bathe in our own greater sunlight. Pyrena is a small world of incandescent gas, blazing purple. You will see our dim purple nights—strangely beautiful.

You are now to proceed as follows:

I attach herewith a rough map of my own, giving the general conformation of Xenephrene's surface. I drew it from my own sketches made as I came down from space. It is of necessity vague and inexact.

These people are not explorers. They know little about their own world. And only a fraction—a very small fraction—of the globe's surface seems habitable. Much of it is fluid . . . not water, not air—you shall see! The vast fluid areas I have marked so on the map. And there are areas of tumbled, jagged mountains of metal—naked metal. And metal plains, smooth and barren as glass.

The country of the Garlands I have plainly marked. As you descend, you will have no difficulty in recognizing the globe's larger fluid area, the larger configurations—and thus in locating, as you come closer, our little land. It is very small—on Earth we would call it some three hundred miles, roughly oval.

We are only a million and a half people here, we of the Garlands. The Brauns are scarcely a hundred thousand. I have marked their one city on the map, where it lies in the northern edge of our domain, with the equatorial mountains and the fluid lake of Tyre and the Tyre plain near it.

Beware this region, Frederick! Come up from the south! I suggest now that you head for our south pole. If you have made the voyage in my calculated time, you will find Pyrena ascending from her southern swing. She rotates in retrograde, at an average distance of eighty-nine thousand miles.

Head for the south pole, within Pyrena's orbital distance. Then come up toward the equator, between our moon and Xenephrene. If you are on time, you will find our moon at the full.

As you descend, you will go into Xenephrene's shadow, with her between you and the sun. It is what I desire—there will be less chance of your being seen. In the area of our night, with Pyrena shining full upon you, descend into our atmosphere. You will find it extends outward some four hundred miles. Take it very slowly, Frederick—be careful of the heat of your descent through it. Judge nothing from now on by Earthly standards! Remember that!

You should be about over our ten degrees south latitude when you descend into the atmosphere. Keep between us and Pyrena—and come north to eight degrees S.

You will be in the night, with Xenephrene rotating under you as you hover. Your altitude now should be about forty miles. If the clouds bother you, descend to keep under them. If the night is too overcast, so that from beneath the clouds Pyrena is lost to you, and the darkness is too great for you to see our surface readily—wait until it clears. Take no chances! Haste of that sort is too dangerous! Let Xenephrene rotate for another day and night. I will see the weather and understand.

When the country of the Garlands comes into view, watch for my light. You will see it—a thin, steady white beam, pointing at the moon. Occasionally I shall send a red flash along its beam, at alternating intervals according to the enclosed code. Thus there can be no mistake. I fear treachery—one fears everything in such times as these we are undergoing here!

When you are convinced it is my light you see, descend toward its source. At an altitude of ten thousand feet, cross into my beam and hold there for a time, that I may see and recognize you. I will send two swift red flashes. Leave the beam at once, and come back into it. I will know for certain then that it is you.

Descend now, down the beam to its source. When

I extinguish it, you will see my glow of lights at your landing field. Descend there and land.

I caution you again. Take everything very slowly! You will be seated, you three, in the lower compartment. Once you are upon solid ground, extinguish all but one very small light. Then begin to open your door.

I say, *begin* to open it! It is to be opened very, very slowly. You Frederick, understand, no doubt, that its strange construction was to some purpose. I was specific about that!

You are to undo its inner fastenings, and revolve its main circular knob a few turns at intervals of no less than five minutes each. I want you to take fully thirty minutes to open the door.

Let the new air of Xenephrene in slowly, that you may grow accustomed to it gradually as it comes upon you. This, of course, you have guessed as my reason for such caution. But it is not only the changed air you will be admitting! Other things will come in as well! To them also, you must become accustomed gradually.

When the door is nearly ready to open wide, extinguish your remaining light. Sit quiet! Do not attempt to move about! Let Frederick rejoin you, when he has flung wide the door. Sit quiet, all three of you. Do not be afraid! There is nothing to fear! It will be strange at first.

I will give you a minute or so to gather your composure. Then I will come in to you.

I pray now, as I close, that all this may transpire as I have outlined! God grant that you will come safely over such a distance! I will be waiting anxiously for that first sight of you in my beacon beam!

Your affectionate father.

My voice trembled and broke as I ended. Emotion swept me—not only an answering love for my father which sprang to meet his as it came from the written words, but a fear as well. And an awe—what was this into which

91

we were plunging that he should be constrained to caution us in such a fashion?

I laid down the letter. Dan did not speak; his questioning eyes were on my face. Freddie said huskily, "Well—" and stopped.

"So," I said. "That's all."

We stared at one another. As though by common consent, with dread we avoided discussion of what now lay before us—the landing, the opening of the door to admit this strange new world. Its air, different from that to which we were accustomed, would come in. *And other things!*

What other things?

The three words gradually came to hold for me an uncanniness almost intolerable. Something not to be faced—yet we would have to face it. "Absurd," I thought. "Why, father is there—and Hulda. And Zetta—"

In truth, it was more an unreasoning dread than fear. For as I examined it I found that, more than anything in life, I desired now to reach Xenephrene and my loved ones. And all the vague, mysteriously uncanny things in the universe could not have served to keep me from them.

"Where's the map?" asked Dan, breaking my disquieted reverie. "Let's look it over."

We examined it: a crude drawing upon animal skin the same as served for father's letter. It seemed very explicit. We were, according to father's calculated time, exactly where his hopes would now be placing us.

If all went well, we would arrive upon one of those nights in the full of the moon during which he would expect us. As he surmised, our small telescope had long since showed us Xenephrene's moon, a tiny blazing point, purple like the planet itself. It showed now, just plunging behind its parent disk: a purple point of light, with its leaping tongues of flame even to the naked eye a quite visible corona.

Our approach to Xenephrene! I might write for hours and barely touch upon the beauty, the splendor, the wonder of it. A purple disk, tingeing with red as we neared it. Convex now—a full, round, glowing world, banked and mottled with clouds, beneath which the faint configurations of its surface-marking gradually became visible.

We headed for its south pole, rounded over it at some fifty thousand miles' distance. We saw over us, hanging to the left, the blazing purple moon. It was night, as father had said, on this moonlit side of the planet. For what would have been an Earth-day of twelve hours or more, we dropped downward into the shadow. The sun was hidden behind Xenephrene now; the moon blazed on us in all its purple glory.

Freddie, during these hours, was busy with constant observations and calculations. Dan and I sat enthralled with the magic of the coloring. As we slid upward toward Xenephrene's equator and gradually descended, the planet's rotation showed quite visibly under us.

The time came when all the visual heavens beneath us were encompased by Xenephrene's bulk. There were at the moment but few clouds to hide its moonlit surface.

"Here," said Freddie: "Take a look."

He had been gazing through the floor window with a telescope. I took it, and gazed upon a purple area of what seemed a liquid haze. To the left was a jagged mountain range, naked crags of gleaming metal in the moonlight. To the right, and extending far up to the rim of the northern horizon, stretched a vast, glassy plain, smooth, motionless as a frozen sea congealed. It gleamed like burnished copper in a purple light. It seemed devoid of even a grain of sand, a twig, a blade of grass. But there was one place where, in a depression, water seemed to have gathered—an irregular crescent sea perhaps a hundred miles in length. I mentioned it to Freddie.

"Yes," he said. "I've identified it on the map. We're on the other side now from the Garland country, as your father calls it. He's in the daylight now."

"Then tonight—" Dan began.

"Yes, tonight. Approximately eleven hours from now, our landing place should be under us. We're eighteen degrees S now and I'll swing us up to ten degrees S, and we'll wait."

93

The full moon held level above us. As the hours passed, while we gently dropped downward, cloud areas began forming beneath us.

Freddie set his jaw. "I'm going down—this is the night he'll expect us. If the clouds will break away—"

They did. We descended into Xenephrene's atmosphere. Our tiny globe grew intolerably hot; then Freddie slowed us, and we kept the cold air circulating. We went through the clouds. A dead purple mist, and then they broke above us. A rift of moonlight came through. Land beneath us! We could see it: a vague moonlit landscape, far down.

Freddie was at the telescope constantly; Dan and I worked the controls at his direction. Forty thousand feet, Eight South Latitude. We were hovering in the dark over a rolling country of what seemed trees perhaps—all vague and blurred and purple.

"Know where we are?" I asked anxiously.

"Yes. Over the Garland country. The south middle of it, I should say. That Braun city he mentioned—I got a glimpse of it, Peter. Up to .the north. We're all right—if only his light would show!"

Then we saw his light! A thin, motionless white beam, standing up into the clouds, where occasionally the full moon broke through a rift. His light! We were sure of it presently. A red wave of color started from its source at the ground and flashed upward. Then another, and others, at intervals. We timed them: compared them to father's notations.

The time-intervals were correct. It was his welcoming beacon!

Freddie had been keeping us cautiously away. But now at the ten thousand foot altitude he swung us into the light. Its white glare bathed us, came up through our floor window. Presently the two red flashes came; we moved away, then back again, answering father's signal. Then, holding to the light, we slid slowly down its motionless length.

I do not know how long it took. It seemed an hour, while we sat in our lower compartment, with the white glare streaming upon us. Then at last, without warning, the glare vanished.

We had extinguished our interior light. We were left abruptly in darkness.

I heard Dan's perturbed voice: "Freddie, shall I stop us?"

Freddie was on the floor, peering down. I knelt beside him. He called to Dan, "No, let us go. We're still pretty well up."

I half whispered, "Can you see anything?"

It all seemed quite dark for a moment. As though we were dropping into a blank, bottomless pit. Then, as our eyes grew accustomed to the absence of the glare, outlines below began to take form. The moon was gone behind a cloud. But there was enough light left to show us a dark ground, with a faint glow suffusing it, perhaps a thousand feet below us. It seemed a solid, open, flat area, flanked with small hooded lights. Our landing field.

There was nothing else to be seen: the purple darkness crowded everything. The open space was directly under us; Freddie made sure of that. He lighted our smallest portable light, at the controls with his instruments before him, and brought us gently down.

A minute . . . ten minutes. None of us spoke. There was a very slight thump. Our little world trembled, came to rest. We had landed!

Freddie stood up. His fingers wavered slightly—perhaps because of his excitement, and the new solidity beneath his feet which made him momentarily unsteady.

"You sit still—I'll start—I'll start opening the door."

His voice held a quaver. He glanced at the chronometer, crossed the room swiftly, and took a turn or so at the door wheel. A giant shadow of him as he moved fell grotesquely misshapen upon our curved wall.

He came back to us and sat down. "Nothing to do now but wait."

The minutes passed in silence. We did not speak. At intervals of five minutes, Freddie made his noiseless trip to the door and back. My heart seemed nearly smothering me. Cold beads were dank on my forehead, neck and chest.

Waiting for the unknown to make itself—seen? —heard? —felt? With every sense alert and straining, I sat waiting. Fear? It was that, of course. I am not ashamed of it: there is no man brave enough to confront the unknown with heartbeat undisturbed.

Nothing—as yet. Or perhaps my panting, labored breath was from the new world air which now was coming in? The ringing in my head, the flashes of red in the dimness before my straining eyes—were they caused only by the tenseness of fear?

Freddie sat down beside me. I heard his whispered words, "Peter! It's almost open. One more turn will do it. Dan—you all right? —Peter, I'm scared—actually scared!"

And Dan's gruff answer, "Yes. I'm all right. Go ahead—finish it."

Our side windows were black rectangles. What was out there? For a time, thought of father had left me. *He* was out there. Was he looking in upon us? I could see nothing; but now the thought of father steadied me. And Zetta. Was she here—near me at last?

Freddie snapped out our light with a click, thundering, echoing in the stillness. The darkness leaped upon us. Darkness and silence. But I seemed to hear my beating heart.

And then I realized that this was no silence! Around me came thronging a million tiny noises. Jostling things of sound in the darkness—things all alive with sound! I could hear them murmuring, whispering like wraiths of jabbering things alive with sound. Or *was* it sound I was hearing? It was all so vague, so unreal, it might have been some other sense. But it was gathering strength: jostling sounds were whirling about my ears, beating at me, gathering strength and mingling into a hum—

All in the darkness. But there was no darkness! Shapes of color—moving shapes of sound and color were here, crowding at my elbows. Formless blobs, impalpable as colored shadows; formless, yet I could imagine them into any form I chose. Jabbering, impalpable things pushing at each other

96

as though for a better view of me! Impalpable? Suddenly one seemed to brush me; I could have sworn I felt it, light as a fairy's wing, touching my hand.

It may have touched Dan also. I heard him lunge. He cursed. An ash tray on the table crashed to the floor, and I jumped to my feet. Panic seemed to be surging about us, out of which came Freddie's voice:

"Easy! Sit down, you two! I'll get the door open wide."

His padding footsteps were reassuring, something solid and real for my confused senses to grip. I could see the moving blob of him, tinged red with a faint aura that now suffused everything.

The solid sound, as he unbarred the door, was steadying. The sound of the door sliding on its hinges as it swung wide—

"These damned things." Freddie came back. He laughed, with a strained break—but at least he *was* able to laugh. "God! It's queer! But it's nothing. Hold steady, you two." His laughter seemed contagious: I heard myself laughing too. But was this madness stealing upon me? A chaos of the undefinable jostled us—a wild chaos of unreality in which my confused senses seemed to be whirling away—

"Peter!" Ah! Reality at last!—father's anxious voice, husky with emotion! "Peter! Frederick? Dan? Are you all right?"

Solidity, reality returned. My whirling senses came back to me. Father was here! The solid thump of his heavy step sounded; the solid glow of the purple light he was carrying filled the room. The reality of his voice, his step—and then his arm was around my shoulders!

And I heard Hulda's happy, welcoming laughter. I kissed her, held her in my arms for a moment . . . and all the red shadows and crimson whisperings of a moment before were forgotten.

Then came another voice—timorous, gentle, eagerly friendly—and a lovely small figure in the doorway. Zetta! Her dear, quaint voice which for all these months had been ringing in my memory was sounding now in reality at last!

XI

"UNDER GARDENS"

"WELL!" SAID FATHER. "Well, you did come safely, didn't you? I'm so glad, Peter. Light your light, Frederick. Well Dan! I'm mighty glad to see you. Here's Hulda! Come here, child—here's your Dan at last!"

Freddie snapped on our light. Even in the confusion of our joyous greetings I was aware of how strange father and Hulda looked. Father wore his hair, snow-white now, in a long, thick, shaggy mass about his ears; a smooth and glossy black animal skin was draped about him, with a white decoration on his chest. His arms and legs were bare, with skin sandals on his feet!

And Hulda! Her brown hair was shot now with pure white strands. It fell in waves upon her bare white shoulders, where her filmy robe of light-brown silken fabric was caught with gay red ribbons. The robe hung in folds nearly to her knees.

I have seen pictures of the maidens of ancient Greece. Hulda looked like that. Things of red crossed her breast, bound her waist and hung dangling at her knees with tasseled ends. Her legs were bare, her feet in sandals like father's, but with pointed toes, the heel cut away, and thongs of red crossing her instep. Her right arm was bare. But on the left, her wrist was bound with red ruching.

Dan had enfolded her in his first hungry embrace, kissing her without thought of the rest of us, until she cried for breath. Then he held her at arm's length.

She was gasping and laughing. "Do I—look so queer? Dan, don't you like my looks? Don't you—like me—?"

"Like you?" His great arms would have wrapped her up again, but she fended him off. She was radiant. I can imagine how Dan felt: I had never seen Hulda half so beautiful. She was blushing and laughing.

"The red, Dan." She indicated her tassels, and the ruch-

98

ing at her left wrist. "You see—I wear it for you. The sign that I am spoken for, and pledged to a man."

"Wonderful, Frederick, that you all got through so safely." Father turned from Freddie to me. "Peter, have you seen Zetta? There she is. Come in, child."

Zetta was dressed very much as I had last seen her on Earth. She stood lingering in the vehicle doorway, eager to see us but reluctant to encroach on our family greetings. At father's words, she now shyly approached.

I stammered, "Zetta, I'm—very glad to see you again."

"How do you do, Peter." She held out her hand, and I took it. A confusion was upon me. This moment for which I had longed came and passed. Perhaps, as once before, the barriers of conventionality rose instinctively to hold my emotion in check.

I think it was so with Zetta, too. Our fingers barely touched; but my heart pounded harder, for I heard her murmur, "Be—careful, Peter. Be very careful!" A warning against the power between us! Then I met her glance as she eyed me sidewise. A roguish, impish look. This was a new Zetta—here upon her own world, her real self. Little imp, mocking my confusion with glee! She turned away, toward Freddie.

Father introduced them.

I saw leaping into Freddie's eyes a swift surprise as he neared her, took her hand and shook it cordially. Freddie's nature is wholly different from mine or from Dan's. Whatever surprise he felt, he gave no further sign; he shook her hand heartily, grinned at her, and turned to me still smiling.

"Say, she's a little beauty, isn't she, Peter?" This was the old Freddie, his characteristic breezy boyishness coming back to him now that he was relieved of the responsibility of commanding our voyage. I had not seen him this way since the first dreadful days of the Great Change had come upon us. He added, "You and I are going to be great friends, Zetta."

Her gaze on him was full of undisguised admiration. "Yes," she agreed. "I think, yes."

99

We were ready to start. "Leave everything," said father. "I'll have it guarded, and we're not going far."

He took his lantern, shook it. It seemed to be a translucent animal-bladder, possibly filled with small objects that rattled. The light from it was a glow of phosphorescence. He held it aloft.

"This light is bad, Zetta. Fix it up, will you? Can't they do better than this?"

Strange thoughts to spring to my mind! As Zetta took the lantern and held it near her face, I fancied that she murmured to it. And as though in answer to her command, the purple light grew stronger! Or at least I fancied so.

"Thanks," said father. "Give it to me; I'll lead the way. Put out your light, Frederick. You lads took your landing very well. Strange and disturbing, isn't it, Peter?—this unreality just beyond our reach. You'll grow used to it— you'll forget it."

He started away, with the rest of us following in the shadows behind his upheld lantern. At his words, the crimson murmuring things in the darkness again began crowding me. But I was not afraid of them now.

On Earth, always there are a million tiny sounds, audible if we will but listen, and things constantly to be seen which, through habit, we look at but cease to see. This was becoming like that. With attention upon it, this unreal sub-world of Xenephrene was strange and fearsome. But it never obtruded. And already, as father said, I found myself ignoring it.

There was, indeed, so much of strange reality spread now before me! We stepped from our small doorway, upon the solid ground of Xenephrene. The moon was beneath a heavy cloud. The landing lights were extinguished: darkness enveloped us. It seemed a haze; the swinging purple rays of father's lantern showed it as a swaying mist in the air.

The night was warm, almost steamingly oppressive. But this feeling, too, soon passed, and I found it wholly comfortable. The lantern, I learned later, was what I had thought—filled with phosphorescent insects like fireflies. And Zetta had commanded them to shine more brightly!

100

Father led us slowly. The ground was level beneath my feet—a corrugated, metallic surface. Sometimes there seemed a soil, and in the darkness, the deeper shadows of vegetation. Great leaves arched up over us, and soon we were under them, walking now on a soft, moldy turf. A heavy, earthy scent rose from it: the damp smell of molding vegetation. In the air too there seemed to be the scent of distant blossoms, a fragrance which seemed to lie in strata, for occasionally it was heavy, exotic.

A moving shadow came up to us—a white-skinned man, darkened by the purple glow of father's light.

"Oh, Kean?"

"Yes, Professor." He spoke our language!

"We're going down. They came safely. Have the guard placed as I directed."

"Yes, Professor."

"Come to me after sunrise, Kean. I'll have plenty to discuss then."

They passed a man, skirting in the shadows. Kean said, "They are checking too many of the Brauns in. A hundred or more came tonight."

Father murmured, "That's bad. Very bad."

Zetta said quickly, "That woman, Brea—and I saw her today—"

The fellow Kean seemed a young man, my own age or less. His face was serious. "Yes, I saw her. They checked her in—for how long it is they would let her stay, I do not know. Too many Brauns are here now. They come, but there seems no record of their going—"

"Place the guard," said father. "And after sunrise I'll see you, Kean."

Zetta murmured, "Kean, will you seek out Graff? I wish to see him—talk to him—"

"No," said father flatly. "You know how I feel about your efforts—the futility of trying to influence that scoundrel—"

"But yes," she said quietly. "I would try once more." A clinging, soft little vine, I had thought her, but obviously it was not so. She dared to defy father. Kean met father's glance. Evidently he also did not approve of Zetta's request.

101

"I may not see him," he returned evasively.

Before Zetta could speak again, he vanished silently into the shadows. I fancied he made a leap upward. I did not see him come down. We started off.

We were now descending down a gentle slope. The verdure grew thicker as we advanced. The perfume in the air turned aromatic, as though scented by a million spiced blossoms. Abruptly the moon came out for a moment, a small purple sun. The darkness lifted. We were in a jungle of vegetation. It arched over us—great, leafy spires, interlocking to a network through which the moonlight straggled.

There seemed to be few trees: it was all a network of stalks, and giant vines and great huge lacy leaves. Pods and flowers hung in clusters. Over our heads the foliage was solidly interwoven. I gazed up, and in the open moonlight up there on top of this tangled vegetation it seemed to me that an artificial roadway—a street perhaps—was resting. There were moving shapes up there, as though people might be passing along a city street.

"Here we are," father called back over his shoulder. He shook his lantern vigorously, and raised it over his head. "Here we are: 'Under Gardens,' Hulda named it. Our home —yours too, now, while we are here." He chuckled. "You might almost think you were back on Earth."

He had stopped to let us come up with him. We had been following a narrow, winding path, which like a tunnel had been cut downward into the jungle. It opened now unexpectedly into a small clearing. Rather should I call it a cave. The vegetation obviously had been hewn away to form a circular opening, a cleared ground space in an oval of a few hundred feet, walled in by the jungle with the heavy network closing overhead fifty feet or more above us.

The moonlight straggled down, to mingle its purple light with father's purple lantern. I saw here, in this cave-like space, a small house built in Earth-fashion, a solidly square, two-storied structure of metallic rock blocks. Its walls gleamed smooth and burnished. Its windows had shutters sticking out at an angle. Behind one of the windows a dull interior light showed.

102

There was a front veranda with a railed balcony over it. Flowers were massed upon a flat roof. A few of their stalks had climbèd and mingled with the vegetation arching above the house. On the ground there was a front garden with a metallic fence. There were flowers growing, and low things in the ground which might have been vegetables.

Altogether, it was a friendly-looking little dwelling place, neat, orderly and, for all its fantastic surroundings, of wholly Earthly aspect. It was, for that reason I think, as surprising a sight as anything I ever saw on Xenephrene.

Father lost his grimness long enough to smile at our amazement. "The government built it for me. They were very kind—then. They built it exactly as Hulda and I directed. I'm sure they think it's the most bizarre affair in the world."

We were at the garden gate, which father had flung open. He sighed heavily. "If we could have been welcoming you at a time less critical, less frightening—Xenephrene is really very beautiful, Dan."

We mounted the metallic veranda and entered the living room. It held a soft illumination of yellow-white light. There was grass matting on the floor, and a polished wooden table with queerly porous wood. On the table was a lamp of skin like the lantern father was carrying. His writing materials were there too.

Furniture stood about the room, chairs, a metallic bowl with water and flowers. On the floor was a huge cushion bound with a fabric rope. I surmised it to be a seat for Zetta.

Father gazed abstractedly around him but I felt his thoughts were far away from the tranquil scene before him.

When next he spoke, his voice was almost a mumble. He said, "Things have reached a crisis here—so swiftly, like the carpet being pulled from under my feet. I was their friend. They were mine. But now—"

Zetta said swiftly, "My people are making a mistake!"

Father murmured, "Yes. If only they will listen to me tomorrow. But I have no hope that they will. The damage has been done, is being done day by day. . . . But no more of this now. Sleep first, and then we'll plan—whatever is possible. . . ."

His utter hopelessness was contagious. I went to sleep finally, but my heart was heavy and I was filled with ominous fears.

XII

AT DAWN

"WE HAVE AN hour," said father. "There is a great deal I must tell you, but we must make it brief."

"Kean will be coming at sunrise," Hulda said.

Dan looked at her quizzically. "Your hair must have a drug in it, Hulda. What's the matter with it?"

Father interrupted, "Look at mine: wholly white. There's something in the air here—it kills the pigment coloring. There's no one here with hair other than white."

With father and Hulda, we were seated on the roof of Under Gardens.

Hulda served us breakfast in a quaint simulation of the way she would have done it on Earth. I would not pretend to describe the food. There was a beverage which might have been either tea or coffee—a sweetish mixture of some herb; and the cooked flesh of what I hoped was an animal.

"Nice breakfast, Hulda," I said lamely, as we were finishing.

"Come now, we'll go upstairs," father said with an air of urgency.

It was dim on the rooftop. The full moon was evidently low to its setting horizon. Shafts of its purple light slanted down through the thick arch of vegetation. The flat roof of the house had a low metal parapet; paths ran between gleaming basins of flowers and a small open area with comfortable chairs. We seated ourselves and father produced what were evidently home-made cigars. But they were not bad.

Within the vault of this encompassing wall and ceiling of vegetation, the air hung heavy upon us. I had been convinced that a street was overhead. If so, it was untraveled now—in the moonlight up there I could not see any moving figures.

There seemed nothing living in sight. A moment later I was not so sure. Vines ran up like ladders from the rooftop of the house to the jungle ceiling, and far up there I thought I saw a figure of some kind clinging. A brown shape—a man, an animal? Or was it some giant brown insect lying motionless on a great stalk of the vines? And then, down on the ground in front of the house by the front fence, I saw unmistakably a brown crawling thing. The length of a man, crawling prone with several legs. It raised an eye toward our roof: a spot of dull red light with a circle of smaller lights around it.

I stared! It came crawling to the gate, raised itself up, standing erect the height of a man upon a tripod of jointed legs; then sank back and crawled slowly on, following the line of fence.

"That—that thing," I gasped finally. "Did you see it?"

Father laughed. "One of our guards. We've half a hundred of them on the ground here and in the foliage. We're alarmed over Zetta's safety. We've every reason to be—"

This gave me my chance. "Where is Zetta?" I asked.

Hulda said, "She'll be here any moment now. I didn't want to awaken her."

Father settled himself in his chair. There was a sort of breathlessness about him as he started talking, as though there was much to be said, with little time in which to say it:

"Before I can make you understand conditions here, I'll have to give you an idea of the history of this world, this race of human beings so unlike ourselves physically, yet in their human qualities so similar. Don't fidget, Fred; I know what you want are the cold scientific facts and problems. I'll be as brief as I can.

"They have always called Xenephrene 'The Wanderer'.

105

It was their name for their world. Our ancient Earth astronomers termed our planets of the Solar System 'wanderers'. Of course they are not. They are chained to our sun, as you know. But Xenephrene had always been free, wandering free from all the stars. Thus you will understand that the astronomical conditions we have here now are all new to Xenephrene. What they were before is immaterial: nights of wan starlight, purple days of Pyrena's moonlight.

"Very little of Pyrena's surface is habitable and there is only one main race, these Garlands, and only this one habitable region. They call it and the city here 'Garla'. Ten thousand years ago the Garlands were evidently a very progressive people. Their records show it. The Garlands had passed that era of development which we on Earth had attained before this catastrophe struck us. Their traditions speak eloquently of a past age when they lived in a machine-made world of science. Not far from here is the ruined shell of one of their cities. It is abandoned, in ruins now.

"But they found, strangely enough, that these labor-saving devices, this artificial existence, complex, automatic, did not bring happiness. They found out, these Garlands, they were on a wrong track! It may have taken them centuries to become fully convinced of it. But slowly through these years, the machines began to decay, modernity to vanish as they slipped back to the simple life.

"They had the knowledge to wrest from nature a comfortable existence. As their wants grew fewer, they looked at each other not like mistrustful, predatory animals, but with a new kindness.

"But there is evil nature here, as everywhere. The Garlands have preserved enough of their science to enable them to control it. There is a scientific body—they call it by a word I translate as Guild. It's a small body of scientists, wholly trustworthy. Their work is secret, so that no ambitious individual may have access to it."

I interrupted, "Or at least you hope so! But, these crimson things—this sound—"

It was around us, murmuring in our ears.

"It is harmless," he said. "If controlled."

It was what his look implied that made me shudder.

Dan put in, "What's the problem? If there's no stress, no struggle—"

"In fundamentals, that is true. But the human equation— that never varies. The good, and the evil."

Freddie said urgently, "But there must be two races here. You mentioned the Brauns in your letter. Are they the race which menaces the Earth?"

"I'm trying to tell you. There was only one race here, the Garlands. A large percentage of them wanted to give up modernity, but a minority did not. Out of this diversity the Garland rulers tried to separate the discordant element. Generations ago it was found expedient to exile criminals to a region north of here, at the edge of the metal plains. Criminals were banished there, and there they bred their kind. Later, it was made by law a crime to preach modernity. The element who still lusted for the old achievement were classed as criminals and banished also.

"The Garlands are the ruling race. They are infinitely more numerous than the Brauns of this exile territory. The Brauns are not allowed here except when they are checked in through our frontier guards. Their government is despotic actually, ruled by a fellow named Graff, a giant of a fellow who calls himself a scientist. He is a genius in his way. It is he who menaces Earth."

Earth! at the mention of it, with the chaotic condition I knew existed there, the apathy of the people, the disintegration of its defences, its scientists, its normal leadership, my fears and impatience became almost unbearable.

"Where is this fellow Graff?" I exploded. "Who is he—?"

"You'll see him," my father said. "Certainly he has a genius for organization. A magnificent physique. He can sway people, a great orator. He has talked himself to where he is: the most powerful influence, very probably, on Xenephrene. But we mustn't despair. There is still slight hope." His voice fell to almost a whisper. "It is largely up to me and my own power of persuasion—and the basic good judgment of the Garland people themselves."

107

Father hesitated, then leaned forward toward us. "I come now to the more recent events which concern us directly. Xenephrene wandered in to join our family of planets gathered about our sun. Graff, with his science, was well aware of what had happened. His magna-telescope showed him our Earth—and apparently showed him things on Earth that gave him a lust for conquest.

"He gathered a small force and went to Earth. Not to conquer—the trip was experimental. He landed, as we know, near New York."

"Zetta—" I began."

"Zetta and her father were here in Garla. Zetta's father, alone of all the Garland government, was anxious to stop him. He preached against the invasion, even in its preliminary form. He wanted to protect the Earth people, or at least to warn them. Zetta felt the same. Her mother is dead; she and her father were very close to each other. This swaggering fellow Graff fell in love with her."

"In love with her!" I exclaimed.

"Yes. He has pleaded for her many times. He never comes here without pleading with her to return to the Braun city with him. He's very gentle with her: she seems not to fear him. She tries to bargain with him, telling him she will give herself to him if he will give up his ambition to conquer the Earth. She would sacrifice herself for us and for what she considers the ideals and good of her own people!"

"He's in Garla now?" I asked.

"Yes. Graff's expedition to attack Earth is now ready. He is here in Garla buying food. And when I think of the outposts of our area of supposed safety on Earth—crumbled, completely ineffectual under the weight of changed climate and human distress—when I let myself think of it—"

"Who is Brea?" I asked.

"A woman, in love with Graff. But he does not love her. He loves Zetta."

"You were telling us of Zetta's trip to Earth," Freddie prompted.

"Yes. Her father was with her. They could get no help from the Garlands, who were beginning to listen to Graff's propaganda. Only the Scientific Guild supplied them with their vehicle. But this same Guild now treats me as an outsider. I don't know of all the weapons they may have. As to Graff's method of attack on Earth—there is the 'Crimson Sound'. It is allied with the infrared world."

"Zetta's father died on reaching Earth," Hulda added. "He had been ill, and it was all too much for him. Then Zetta determined to carry on alone."

"Yes," father agreed. "And Graff knew she was on Earth. He came to get her. I was up and Hulda awake. The man Graff sent captured all three of us. We went back in the vehicle Zetta arrived in. Our captor's name is Kean—that same young fellow who spoke to us last night. He has become our trusted friend. He had been swayed by Graff's oratory, but that's over. Now he's on our side."

XIII

"EMPEROR OF THE EARTH!"

KEAN TOOK ME to one side. He said in a low voice, "We must take more care of Zetta. They have not told you. Brea, the woman, attempt' to have her murdered."

My temples began to throb; the sudden speed of my heartbeat seemed to stifle me. "My God—" was all I could mutter.

Father was saying, "I'm going before the Council at noon. Kean, tell them I'm bringing my son and two young friends."

"Yes. The people are excited, interest' that men of Earth are here. But most interest' in Graff. He promises much to them."

I whispered to Dan, "Father said you'd have to ask Hulda why Kean brought his captives here instead of delivering them to Graff. He had been convicted falsely of a crime, and he was bitter about that. But the case was re-opened and he was exonerated. That's not the reason for his change of heart, though."

109

"Why, then?" Dan demanded.

"Because he's fascinated by Hulda. Look at him now." Dan's expression was a study. "Well, you can't blame him, can you. . . ."

Kean prepared to leave presently; and Dan made a studied attempt to be friendly. Kean's handclasp was firm and cordial, his gaze into Dan's eyes unfaltering. He carried himself then, and indeed always, with a manly dignity worthy of anyone's admiration.

When he was gone, Hulda turned to Dan, flung her arms about his neck and kissed him.

The morning was well advanced when we started with father from "Under Gardens". Just as we were starting, Freddie said:

"Professor Vanderstuyft, fix it so we can go through the Scientists' Grotto, will you?"

"Yes. There are things to be seen. I want you to see the Infrared Control. This I was already permitted to see: the greatest power for good or evil in this world."

A group of the brown insect things were ranged before our gate! I could not approach them at first without an inward shudder. Jointed brown things crawling prone on the ground—gruesome. Not only because their size was fully that of a man, but gruesome in the way they sometimes stood upright upon three hind legs, their other legs dangling like arms, heads grotesquely wearing a single, multiple-lens eye, antennae waving above their heads.

Gruesome for all this and more gruesome for a crude leather jacket strapped around them in the fashion of a garment. Things—living things—more than giant insects as we of Earth would conceive the term. Yet less than humans.

Some stood erect now. They eyed my father as one to whom they must look for commands. Others crawled unheeding along the edge of the fence. Ghastly! One stopped, half raised itself and eyed me with a calculating stare that turned me cold.

We started. Some of the insects remained around the house. Eight went with us, four of them slithering along on each side. It was full daylight now. The sunlight came down through the jungle ceiling in a subdued glow. There *was* a street up there: I could see the straight lines of a causeway laid upon the top of the foliage. Figures moved along it: people so incongruously light of weight that they made hardly a flutter as they passed by.

We were under a portion of the city. Father had said so. Now, almost at once, we came to the foot of an incline which led us upward.

We left the solid ground. The inclined causeway upward was some twenty feet wide and made of porous tree-trunks, lashed together with heavy vegetable fiber. The whole structure bent and swayed beneath our weight.

Shortly we had climbed it and had reached the heart of the city called Garla. A crowd already was gathering, the people staring at us silently. Father waved them away, and gave a murmured, queer guttural command to our insect convoy. The things dropped down, lay quiet in a group.

Near at hand, on a tree-trunk framework, was a small platform some twenty feet in the air, with a ladder leading up to it.

"Come up," said father. "We can see better from there."

We mounted, and gazed upon as strange a scene as ever I could have imagined. The surface of Xenephrene here was covered for an area of perhaps five miles square with this dense forest growth. Its top, two hundred feet above the ground, was tangled and matted into an undulating surface.

Upon this forest top, the main section of the city of Garla was built. The streets—we seemed to be on one of the main ones—were narrow crooked roadways of split porous logs, bound with matting. The tops of the jungle vines projected with waving branches between them.

Father commented, "Nothing living weighs very much here. All organisms seem constructed with strange lack of solidity." Zetta, both on Earth and Xenephrene, weighed some eighteen pounds!

There were white-faced, white-haired half-naked children gazing now at us from the nearby houses. Women passed

111

us—in aspect, save for their flowing white hair, they were not unlike our country women before the Great Change. But these women weighed twenty or twenty-five pounds. Strange phenomenon! The men of Garla wore crude leather garments; they were bare-legged, bare-armed, with white hair flowing about their ears. These men might weigh about thirty pounds.

All flimsy! Everything flimsy. It brought a sudden sense of hope and feeling of power. Why, in a hand-to-hand struggle I could smash a dozen of these men! We of Earth were solid. The platform bent beneath our weight. No wonder father had requested his home be built down where it was!

I have not pictured the strangest aspect of all. The city was busy with its activities. There seemed no vehicles here —pedestrians only, moving about their daily tasks. Strange, weird movements! They walked along the streets in easy graceful leaps, fifteen feet at a stride.

Hulda touched my arm. "That open area, with the curved line of branches standing up—that's what might be called their stadium."

Zetta added, "Graff speaks there to the people tonight."

"It's a frightening thing," father said musingly, "what one evil man can do. These people were content, kind, unselfish until this man rose up among them. Now conflict, argument, and dissension have been aroused. Everywhere here, friction and questioning uncertainty, where so short a time ago, there was a tranquility, a simple happiness!"

We presently descended from the platform. Father explained the intertwining interests of the Brauns and the Garlands and, however much the Garlands might question Graff's motives and actions, the two races actually had their interests closely interwoven. And it was we, the foreigners, who were the aliens, now.

When father first arrived, they had respected him and listened to his advice. But gradually the power of Graff's oratory, his sweeping personality, his incessant propaganda, had its effect. As this evil genius rose in power, father and his influence waned.

Strange walk we had that morning through the city

of Garla! Insect workers were everywhere—patient, silent, methodical as well-trained domestic animals, yet with a far higher intelligence. I gazed at what might have been a double line of giant red ants, carrying boxes down an incline into the forest.

Patient workers? But I was struck with the feeling that there was a sullen resentment upon them; a smoldering resentment and hate for their masters.

Father pointed out a few Brauns, swaggering and flushed with their new sense of importance. At sight of them the cynical thought came to me that in clothes and manner they might have been a burlesque of us on Earth. They eyed us with hostile stares.

Kean approached. "The Council refuse to see any but you, Professor," he said. "An' they say they give no decision until after Graff' meeting tonight!"

Dan spoke up. "The idea is, if the Garland public is enthusiastic about Graff's invasion, they'll turn us down—give us no help whatever to save Earth! Isn't that it, Kean?"

A commotion near us checked his answer. Zetta murmured, "Graff!"

A huge figure of a man was coming slowly across the street, with a half-admiring, wholly awed throng of the Garlands around him. He saw us, waved the crowd back and, with an effortless leap over the thirty feet of intervening street, he stood before us.

Our insect guards rose upright, eyed father, and stood alert. Behind me I saw three young Garland men, with metal objects like small projectors in their hands. Government street guards. They were watching Graff narrowly.

He had learned English, I had been told, from one of his captives when he was surveying conditions in the United States. He now said: "Professor Vanderstuyft—" His manner was courteous, but authoritative. "I would speak with Zetta—one moment."

The man who was about to try to conquer our Earth! I stood tense, and an awe of which I was secretly ashamed swept me briefly as I gazed at him. A giant fellow, six

113

and a half feet tall at the very least. Broad-shouldered, slim-hipped, straight and muscular.

He wore a tubular leather garment, strapped in at the waist and falling like a short flaring skirt to his bare knees; there was a short, gaudy jacket over it. His shoes had broad flat heels and pointed toes, curled up and fastened to his ankles with ornamental metal chains. A heavy metal triangle hung at his chest; chains of gleaming metal hung from his shoulders to his elbows; his muscular forearms were bare, with heavy metal bands at the wrists. A metal band circled his forehead, with the close-clipped white hair under it.

He was a man of perhaps forty years, with deep-set blue eyes, heavy white eyebrows, a beardless face. A strong, handsome face. He was smiling now, but I could see a ruthless determination in the set of his square, cloven jaw, and more than a hint of cruelty in the lines of his thin, firm lips. A swaggering, arrogant fellow. But he was more than that. In his voice, in his bearing, I read a consciousness of his own power: a dignity about him, more than a mere arrogant swagger. A kingly scoundrel, contemptuous by instinct of all his fellow men.

"Zetta," he said. "I am tomorrow going to Earth. I would conquer it for you. Won't you come with me? You are master of yourself by the laws here."

Zetta burst out, "What you plan to do on Earth is wrong, Graff. If you think to please me and—and win my love, stay here! Stay here on Xenephrene!"

He answered her gently, "You are misled, Zetta. You live with Earth people, you begin to think like Earth people. They mislead you. Zetta, come with me on this great conquest—"

"No," she said. "It is evil. You know I call it evil. You want me to love you. You go for that in the wrong way."

Regret swept his face. If this was acting, it was a good brand. Then slowly, amusement, tinged with a faint irony, showed in his glance and his words:

"You do not know it, but when I've succeeded, you will be proud of me. You will see in me the fearless conqueror.

An' everything I have fought for and won, it will be yours!"

Zetta said, "I am finish. I say no more."

He swung from her, head held high. His gaze roved over me as I stood, conscious of my clenched fists; Freddie beside me; Dan towering over us, yet shorter than Graff. Of Hulda, half afraid, clinging to Dan. And Kean, a little apart. Graff fastened on Kean and his thin lips twisted with contempt.

"Ah, there is my little traitor!"

I saw Kean stiffen. For an instant I thought he would hurl himself bodily upon his accuser.

But father interrupted this exchange. He said, "Enough of this. Come Zetta—all of you."

As we started away, again Graff's glance swept us. "So these are some more of my little Earth enemies? Look well upon me! I am Graff, future Emperor of the Earth."

Then he turned slowly and with a lazy bound vanished down the cross street.

XIV

BRAVE, FOOLISH LITTLE ZETTA!

IT WAS A crowded day, with our morning walk through the city and our meeting with Graff. And from a distance, we had seen the woman Brea—an arrogant giantess. A fitting mate for Graff, no doubt. She was already calling herself "Empress of the Earth". Kean informed us she was going to address the meeting tonight, to tell the people of Garla what wonderful things would be brought back to them by Graff when he returned.

Father visited the Garland Council. He returned discouraged and indignant. They would have none of our pleas for them to restrain Graff. Politely, they requested father to leave their politics alone. They repeated that only after Graff's meeting would they give us their decision.

115

"I warned them, they will sacrifice their ideals to no good for themselves or their people. Graff is treacherous, without honor, without loyalty to any except himself. A wholly selfish, unscrupulous scoundrel. They'll see—when it is too late—"

But Freddie, Dan and I were far more interested in how we might personally prevent the impending catastrophe to Earth. We could rely on no one but ourselves. Time was short. Father, with his liking and sympathy with these people of Garla, was slow to move and to condemn.

Dan said, "Even he can't see them as they are, recognize the change that has come over them. Doubtless, when he arrived, they were altruistic, peace loving, all that he told us. But humans are humans. The greed was not dead in them—only dormant, waiting to be aroused. This government is humoring your father, even while it is scheming to get whatever it can out of Graff. Stalling him, delaying any action by him—"

We had moved to one side, where father could not hear us. I said, "You're right. Kean is the only one we can trust. And, of course, Zetta."

Father's mission to the Council having been a complete failure, we returned to our house. What father's emotions were, I do not know. But I do know the rest of us were filled with frustration, a kind of panic at our inability to act, a loss of confidence in father's ability to guide us, a sense of floundering when positive and swift action was essential.

Later in the day, it was Kean who started the constructive thinking. He said he had never been to the Scientists' Grotto, had never seen the weapons, though he knew where they were kept, under heavy guard. But he thought that during the evening meeting Graff was to hold, he would be able to plan a way to get into the arsenal grotto. With the physical force we of Earth were capable of using, we could break into it.

During the meeting, attention would all be centered there. Most of the guards would be at the meeting. Kean planned to investigate conditions at the arsenal and report to us. If

116

we could get the weapons—all except the Infrared Control, upon which Garla was dependent for survival—and get them to our vehicle, then we would try attacking Graff first, here in Garla. Or, as Kean suggested, catch him on his way to the Braun city. Then, if we brought the wrath of the Garlands upon us, we would all escape to Earth.

We said nothing to father, Zetta or Hulda.

Father had arranged for us to go to the grotto during the afternoon. This would give us a preliminary view of its setup before the evening, when Kean would get last minute details. Father took an hour, before our departure, to tell us more of the science of this strange world.

The basis of all natural scientific phenomena on Xenephrene was an entity called *Reet*. An "etheric fluid". A "movement of detached electrons". He used both phrases. In its essence, he said, Reet was an enigma, a force something like our electricity. It existed in nature—in the rain, the clouds, the air. But it was also the growing, life-giving essence of all vegetable and animal organisms.

Just as we of Earth had learned to harness electricity in a wide variety of forms, so on Xenephrene Reet was harnessed. On Earth a common electrical current, a bolt of lightning, a magnetic field, fluorescence of a Crooke's tube, the heat of an electric coil, a giant, leaping electric spark, X-rays —all are akin. On Xenephrene, a score of scientific phenomena were all manifestations of Reet, in various forms, under various abnormal conditions.

Father told us how our vehicle operated. The force of gravity itself is merely a vibration flowing between two material bodies, connecting them with a tendency to draw near, to coalesce—a fundamental tendency in all nature when in vibratory contact. The Reet current, applied in a form abnormal to nature, slows down and stops this gravitational vibration.

It is, to me at least, a deep subject. I leave it to father's text books. But with several of the Reet rays, we were to have diabolical dealings! Their control of the hidden, unseen forces of nature—we saw a little of it that afternoon in the Scientists' Grotto.

117

The grotto, at least this one to which we were admitted, seemed to be a series of underground passages, converging into a number of underground rooms: workshops, laboratories, storehouses—perhaps of weapons and equipment of war. We were shown none of that. We saw, indeed, but one room—but that was enough to leave us shuddering.

On the ground, beneath the forest, we came to the tunnel entrance. A guard—a man standing there, with half a dozen of the insect things lying watchfully beside him—passed us in. We went through a downward sloping tunnel with smooth metallic walls gleaming weirdly in the shifting purple and red lights. There was steady movement of artificially controlled air for ventilation . . . vague, pungent smells . . . and in the distance ahead of us, the murmur and throb of machinery.

It was like plunging into yet another brand new world. Outside the grotto, the Garlands seemed a primitive, pastoral race. This was like a trip centuries into the future. An inferno of the future!

From a cross tunnel, the sudden whine of a dynamo tore at us. A wave of gas, not unlike chlorine, brought us up gasping and choking, until a blast of fresh cool air fortunately dissipated it. We were in a place of shifting lurid lights; workmen passed us, sometimes with masks, but all wearing what seemed to be heavy insulated garments.

An inferno, frightening in its strangeness. Frightening, also, in another way. The half-seen world of the infrared had never left my consciousness since I first set foot upon Xenephrene. It was with me all that morning in the upper streets of Garla, but I had ignored it.

Here, in the gloom and weirdness of the grotto, the crimson chattering things seemed to gain reality. When once we entered the tunnel, I was newly and more acutely conscious of them, as though this were their home, their very breeding place. Or was it their jail? The jail where they were imprisoned, guarded—watchful of any chance for escape? Sullen, resentful!

My nerves were taut, my imagination keyed to its highest pitch. An insect loitered, idly, against the burnished tunnel wall. A purple ball of light was over it. I fancied the thing tensed itself as though to spring upon me. I did not breathe again until we were past it.

A scientist was leading us now—Freddie, Dan, myself and father. We had left the girls at home. We came to the barred entrance to a room. Its door was of heavy metal—nothing flimsy here.

My heart sank. Kean had said that with our great physical strength we might be able to force our way!

A scientist met us. He smiled gravely at father, whom he apparently knew from previous encounters. He was a short slim man, garbed in smooth, dull black. His white hair was clipped close; heavy bulls'-eye goggles made his face grotesque. His ears were clasped with a device which looked a bit like a radio headphone. He removed it, stepping over its dangling wires as he laid it aside.

"Come in," father said softly to us. "This is the control room. I want you to see it."

A low, black-vaulted room. I could see nothing but a small railed area on a two-foot metal platform in the center of the room. Within this low metal railing, on a bare flooring of burnished metal, two small mechanisms stood side by side: two transparent globes, each about a foot in diameter. Within one was a fluorescence of purple; the other held a crimson glow. Wires connected them to nearby batteries. Other wires ran to a bank of indicators—dials and pressure gauges. Above the neck of each globe, fastened to it, was a small grid of wire. From one globe a vague, violet-purple beam streamed out. From the other, the beam was crimson.

I could barely see the scientist as he moved about us. There was no light save these purple and crimson beams.

The man seemed to be adjusting his goggles and replacing his headphone. Then he moved a switch, and the crimson globe sprang into greater intensity. The beam from it deepened: it seemed to stream out across the room, through the further wall of metal rock—opening to my gaze a blackness of distance unfathomable.

A murmur was coming from it—a myriad tiny growls

119

and screams! The crimson sounds! The red things lurking around me responded to it! Or were they making the sounds? I could not tell. They seemed rushing out from the unseen into visibility—searching— One seemed almost to be plucking at me!

Father murmured, "It is bringing the infrared nearer to us. Or swinging us nearer to it—all the same. Bringing the two planes closer together, by whatever means. That ray permeates the whole of Xenephrene—like a broadcasted radio wave on Earth, in a way. But more so. If it persisted —a day, even an hour—the infrared would be let loose upon us. Possessing us!"

The scientist was saying. "Let one of them try it out. This is a very weak intensity."

"Try it, Peter." Father drew me forward. "Stand there in the red glow for just a moment. If you feel too queer, come back out."

Every instinct in me revolted. But I yielded to him as he pushed me gently into the red glow. It bathed me with a tingling warmth. Or was it burning?

The red things were howling around me. One came up— a great crimson shadow. It seemed to be condensing into the form of a man. Suddenly I heard myself laughing. Why, this was funny. It looked like me! A crimson shadow of Peter. Or was it my evil spirit? Its face, malignant, like some diabolical travesty of my own, came close and leered at me. It was trying to get into my body! I laughed, but I was thinking: "Why, this is actual madness—"

Father's hands jerked me back into the darkness. I stood trembling; my face and hands were flushed, as though inflamed.

"Madness indeed," said father, and then I knew that I had shouted the words aloud. "They think that the infrared is perhaps the evil nature of man held submerged. A greater intensity of the criminal sound would have scorched you."

I recalled how Freddie and Dan had been burned in their fight with the intruder that night the cylinder had arrived. I said, "And a still greater intensity would reduce you to the plane of the infrared—dissolve you into nothingness. That must have been the fate of Davis and Robinson, when they attacked the crimson sound near New York—remember?"

The scientist moved back the switch; the red glow faded. Father nodded. Then he said:

"On Earth we have no such condition, but here on Xenephrene, the subworld is always striving for mastery. The purple glow from Pyrena is nature's adjustment. It holds in check the sub-red world. But since Xenephrene came into sunlight, things are changing. Our sunlight seems to be favorable to the infrared. So an artificial adjustment has to be made. The purple haze you see in Xenephrene's air—it all comes from this little globe."

The purple globe now was active; the beam deepened. Around me the red things seemed to vanish. A great peace, a stillness came to the vaulted room. I had not realized under what subconscious strain I had been laboring until it was removed.

Freddie said, "Why use the crimson ray at all? Why not just the purple ray, and banish the red things completely?"

"The red-world cannot be banished completely here on Xenephrene," father answered. "Too great a use of the purple would swing the planet too far toward the ultra-violet, and that would be injurious to human life. The best balance which can be maintained is the purpose of these two globes, this control room."

A solemnity, greater than I had ever heard before, came to father's voice. He said, "The Brauns had no spreading rays on Earth like these. They tell me, here in Garla, that these two small globes are the only ones of their kind in existence. Without them, in a month, or a few months at most, Xenephrene, bathed in our sunlight, would be overrun with the demons of the infrared! It would be a world literally gone mad!"

From our visit to the grotto, we returned home. The insects were quietly patrolling the grounds. The girls were busy about the house.

Hulda whispered to me, "We're getting ready to leave."

"Leave?"

121

"Yes. If you should be successful tonight—if you get the weapons—you might want to leave for Earth at once. Zetta is coming with us; Kean also. Neither has any ties here."

Zetta coming! If only everything would work out!

"Yes, she's coming," Hulda reiterated in answer to my questioning glance. "She's made every effort to save her country from this ambitious tyrant. She knows he would turn on the Garlands as quick as he would crush the inhabitants of Earth. She would even marry him if that would cause him to give up his plans. But she's wiser than you might think. She knows Graff for what he is. She doesn't trust him."

"We must watch her closely, nevertheless, Hulda. Some mad scheme might come to her. She's very young and inexperienced, really."

Hulda agreed and we sat silent, contemplating the hazardous path that lay before us.

XV

GRAFF'S TREACHERY

"It's time," said Hulda. "Shall we start?"

We had been sitting there for almost an hour. It was time now to leave for Graff's meeting. It was our first adventure abroad at night on Xenephrene.

A sense of evil lay heavily upon me. It was a cloudless night, with Pyrena a great purple disk above. The forest was full of purple shadows. The red murmuring things were abroad and I blessed with a new understanding this purple light which held them in check. We ascended the incline and came upon Garla's main street. The two girls were shrouded in cloaks of white, as was father. Once, Hulda raised her cloak like a hood over her head until Freddie asked her to lower it.

"You look like a ghost in this moonlight." He laughed, but it was high-pitched and unlike him.

Dan whispered, "Kean is supposed to join us at the stadium entrance. Do you think he will, Peter? If anything goes wrong—"

"We'll sit near the back," I answered. "He'll find us. You, Freddie and I must sit together, so we can slip away."

Freddie edged toward us as we walked along. The street swayed and bent beneath our weight. "This cursed flimsy city! Peter, give me my knife and revolver. Thank heavens for these dark cloaks."

We three had seen cloaks of a dark woven fiber lying in one of the rooms of Under Gardens. We had wanted to wear them and father had acquiesced.

I raised my cloak and surreptitiously handed Freddie the weapons. We each had a short, wide dirk and an Essen soundless automatic, the only weapons we had brought from Earth.

"Move back," I whispered to Dan. "Father might grow suspicious and want to know what we're talking about."

We were determined to get into the grotto by whatever expedient Kean would think possible of success. Father might approve, but if he did, he would want to go with us. He would be more hindrance than help on such a venture, though, and in the event of failure we wanted him, at least, to remain in safety.

Shrouded in our cloaks, we hastened through Garla's tree-top streets. From over us, as a crowd of young people went past us in a leap, a heavy thing struck Dan on the shoulder. It brought a startled curse from him.

Father was beside him. He said, "I don't like this. In all the months I've been here, this is the first sign of a real hostility." He turned to me and lowered his voice:

"We'll have to try something desperate, Peter. If Graff gets away from us—if he gets to Earth. . . . Whatever can be done to stop him must be done tonight."

I evaded an answer. "Let's hear what he has to say. Kean is to meet us at the entrance."

A Braun went sailing by with a menacing, derisive shout. I called to Dan and Freddie. They came closer, holding our group together. Out of the moonlight Kean came sailing

123

at us, landing lightly beside me. Dan and Freddie stepped closer. I whispered, "It's all right, Kean?"

"Yes. They are remove most of the guards for meeting here. In half an hour, we be ready to try it."

Father approached us. "You coming with us, Kean? The Garlands are hostile. I've never seen anything like it. Have you heard from the border?"

"No," said Kean. "Something is wrong. No Brauns have left. There are very many here in Garla tonight!"

Freddie asked, "Have you seen Graff? Where is he now?"

"Inside," Kean gestured. "On the upper platform leap. The woman Brea is with him, and many Brauns." He whispered aside to me. "Are you guarding Zetta well? After we leave, only the professor will be with her and Hulda, so I order insects—here is one."

An insect appeared upright at our elbows; then another. Kean told father he had ordered them. "Good," said father. "Tell them to stay close to Zetta."

The stadium was a great moonlit area on the tree-top surface. Upon every vantage, people were clinging. In the purple moonlight it was a scene of confusion. The audience was assembling, leaping from the gateway, climbing to look for space.

We entered with our heavy dragging tread. People craned to see us. Some shouted derisively.

"We'll sit here," I whispered to Kean. "Come back as soon as you can."

We took the first empty seats just inside the gate. Platforms and poles partly obstructed our view, but we could see enough. The rostrum from which Graff was to speak was in clear sight. A bank of soft lights up there cast a lurid purple glow which did little more than intensify the moonlight. Brauns were crowded up there; among them I could see the towering figures of Graff and Brea.

We sat in a line, father, Hulda and Zetta at one end, we three conspirators nearer the gate. Behind Zetta, our two insects were lying prone on the surface of a vine. Zetta was next to me. In all the turmoil of my thoughts, I was

124

wholly conscious of it. Her long white hair lay on the seat between us. In the darkness my fingers found a lock of it and clung. She did not know it. Or perhaps she did?· I fancied her shoulder bent toward me.

"Peter," she whispered, "I have arrange with Kean, if you are successful tonight, we all meet you out in the open country, where your vehicle can pick us up—"

An abrupt hush had fallen over the audience. The towering figure of Graff had come to the edge of the platform. He stood etched in the darkness, a lurid purple figure. He raised his arms. He was smiling benignly as he regarded the sea of upturned faces beneath him.

A moment, and then he began to speak. His voice, with its words unintelligible to me, rolled out over the silence— soft, persuasive, yet powerful. Sometimes he turned to regard those behind him. He would speak quietly, then shout a sudden, thundering question. Then a gentle, persuasive question. All the tricks of the true orator! And he was carrying his audience.

Applause broke out. And as it rose in volume, Kean suddenly dropped before me! I looked up to meet his white, agitated face. "Peter, make no sign! Get your father —all of you get out of here!"

Something was terribly wrong! I recall that I felt a slight tug as the lock of Zetta's hair pulled from between my fingers. I forgot it at once, gazing into Kean's horrified face.

A shout stiffened me—an official's voice, bellowing in accents of horror and command.

Kean gasped his news: "The infrared Control! The crimson and purple globes—they have been stolen!"

Up there in the purple moonlight, over the barrage, a black object was descending from the sky. A flying platform —I could not see it clearly. It dropped swiftly down within the barrage circle. In a moment it came sailing up again. It passed high over us. It was a flying vehicle, and the escaping Brauns crowded its rails. The crimson barrage faded out. The rostrum was empty.

Graff's treachery was now laid bare. He had stolen the globes of the infrared Control!

125

Without them, Xenephrene in a month or two was doomed. These frightened officials of Garla, these panic-stricken people, all knew it. A world gone mad! But my thoughts were not concerned with that. The cold horror within me sprang from another source: the realization that Graff had stolen the infrared Control to use on Earth!

My shuddering imagination leaped ahead. Our world, our Earth, gone mad!

XVI

ON HIS WAY TO CONQUER THE EARTH

IN THE CONFUSION I found myself pushed a considerable distance, separated from all our party. From behind me, as I stood there, a dark-cloaked figure darted past me. At first I thought it was Dan, but it was not. It wasn't anyone of Earth. The figure passed through a shaft of moonlight: from the cloak I saw a white arm dangling.

This was a man, carrying someone. In the distance across the city, a siren was sounding, a long, harsh electrical scream.

With the Essen automatic in my hand, I found myself plunging, half falling down the flimsy street. I reached the ground. The moonlight showed clear where the jungle ended and the open country began.

Not pausing for even a moment's caution, I came with a rush out of the dark depths of the forest into an open moonlit area. A red glow hovered like a circular curtain near at hand. Within a dozen steps of me, a small, railed platform lay upon the ground. Men were on it—Brauns! A black-hooded figure was standing holding Zetta!

I must have stood for an instant in confusion. I remember casting off the impediment of my cloak. A dozen men came leaping at me. I raised the Essen to fire but it was knocked from my hand as one of the leaping bodies struck me.

They closed in on me. I turned and swung at them. Flimsy

things! My dirk tore into the shoulder of one of them. He went down with a scream. The dirk had buried, hilt and all—I let it go. I wrenched an arm loose from around my neck, hit another man full in the face. Two others I knocked aside with a sweep of my arm. Another leaped astride my back, but I heaved him off as though he were a tiny child clinging there. They must have been without weapons. They clung, bit and tore · at me—a ring of them struggling to hold me.

I burst through them. But, like birds, they were at me again. I lifted one of them bodily and hurled him a hundred feet. Another I caught by the legs, whirling him as a thirty pound bludgeon to knock the others away.

I had almost reached Zetta. I shouted to her. She answered—but it was a scream of warning. I turned too late. Someone from behind crashed a block of metal stone on my head. I went down into soundless, empty darkness.

When I recovered consciousness I was lying on the platform. It was in mid-air; I could feel it sway, feel the rush of the wind past me on that thirty-foot square, railed platform. Some fifteen men crowded near its center, where, in a small pit, its anti-gravity mechanism was installed. The glow shone upward upon the faces and figures of the seated men—Brauns. I sat up unsteadily. One of my captors was beside me.

The platform was sailing through the purple moonlight. I was too far from the rail to see over it to the ground, but in the distance I could make out a line of the metal mountains, naked crags glistening under the stars.

From behind the platform a yellow fire streamed out like a vessel's wake. We were being propelled forward by the impulse of its thrust against the air. Vertical and horizontal rudders were back there. In front also, and to the sides, were small lateral wing-rudders.

A gentle hand touched my shoulder. Zetta was seated beside me. She was unharmed, her face lighting with relief as she saw that I, too, was uninjured. My head was roaring

127

from the blow. Blood, now drying, matted my hair. But it seemed to be only a scalp wound.

The man moved away from us, facing us but leaving us a chance to whisper to each other. Zetta told me she had been abducted from the meeting but she had not fought to escape.

"You mean you're glad you're here?"

"Yes. It's our last chance. How else is it possible to help my Garla and your Earth?"

There were many other small platforms escaping from Garla. They came presently, converging in upon us.

Zetta pointed. "The border searchlights are gone. Our guards all dead—it was what Kean feared. These platforms came into Garla unseen—taking back the Brauns and what they have stolen."

"The infrared Control globes," I muttered. "They're on Graff's platform undoubtedly!"

Ahead, a great yellow radiance illuminated the sky. The full moon was low to one side of us; to the other the dawn was coming. Almost soundlessly we swept on, over a sea of deep purple water, with a barren metal plain beyond it.

The city came up into view. We saw tremendous metal buildings, set in terraces upon a barren metal rock surface— fantastic structures, aerial like a giant hive. There were spider-web bridges of gleaming metal, giant ladders, metal causeways swinging from cables at heights tremendous—all aerial, spiderlike, fantastically unreal. The city glared with blasts of yellow light, roared with the noises of industry.

We swept over it at a considerable height and dropped into a broad metallic pit in the plain beyond, a pit two hundred feet deep and several miles across. It was flooded with yellow radiance. Brauns crowded close around us; but I caught glimpses of a great activity. At least a thousand men were busy here. Platforms like ours were landing from the direction of Garla. A large one was already here.

Zetta and I were pushed to the ground. A dozen or more space-flying globes of various sizes—somewhat similar to the one Dan, Freddie and I had used coming from

128

Earth—stood about. At a distance, one gigantic affair, a great terraced cylinder with banks of windows like a monster ocean liner, lay on a raised stone platform. Ladders led up to it from the pit-bottom. Our captors nudged us in that direction.

Graff's expedition to Earth was embarking now! I saw very little of it as with a crowd of Brauns around me I was shoved toward the monster vehicle. The sloping ladders had wide steps one above the other at nearly ten-foot intervals. At a word of command, Zetta bounded up.

They let down a cable, hooked it on me, hauled me up the fifty-foot height. I saw them leading Zetta away. She turned toward me, but they forced her on. A Braun threw a metal hook around me, pinning my arms. I was jerked through a doorway, down a long echoing passage, and thrown into a metal room, which had a single bullseye window. The door slammed upon me. I was left alone.

Within an hour, in the light of my second dawn upon Xenephrene, we left the planet and Graff was on his way to conquer the Earth.

XVII

PLANNING THE CONQUEST

"WELL," SAID GRAFF. "I had not thought to have you with me, but it could be for the best."

I got to my feet; I had been lying on the bare metal floor. We were well beyond Xenephrene's atmosphere now. And so insistent are the human mundane needs—even amid all my terror-filled thoughts of Earth's increasing danger—that my chief and most urgent trouble at the moment was an intolerable hunger. "I'd like something to eat—"

"Zetta said you would be hungry," he said. "Well, you shall be fed. Follow me."

He led me down a long metal passage with closed doors

129

along it at intervals. We entered a wide room, set amidship of the vehicle. Through its windows I could see blackness on both sides—the great star-filled void of space.

Zetta was here, perched on a high bench. She flashed me a smile and a warning glance. Food was on the table near her.

"Your breakfast, Peter," she said. "Sit here."

I ate. Strange meal! Strange food of Xenephrene, but stranger still we three as we sat there.

Graff said, "Zetta has ask me to let you live. I would do almos' anything to please her. And with you, she has promise' me you will help with my campaign. You will do this?"

At his brusque question, I hesitated a moment. Then I asked, "How?"

"Information about your worl'," Graff said. "When the time comes, I tell you."

We were twelve days reaching Earth. Dan, Freddie and I had made the voyage in eleven days. In this great ship we were traveling faster, but the distance, with Xenephrene drawing away from the Earth, was greater now.

It was a monotonous, frustrating journey. My weapons had been taken away from me. Three times a day, Graff came personally and took me to that larger room where I found my meal awaiting me. Of all the rest of the ship—its men, its equipment—I saw nothing. I was housed alone in a cabin. This gave me hours of time to plot and scheme. Ironic fact! Until we reached Earth, even the faintest possibility of carrying out the villain's defeat was incredible!

I would whisper these thoughts to Zetta at a time when we were alone. Always she would remind me that the fight for survival, the fight against this onslaught caused by Xenephrene's position in connection with our Earth, was the urgent and imperative need of everyone living on the Earth. The vague whisperings of danger from another planet were lost in the chaos of Earths' readjustments and reconstruction. I must not count on much assistance from the people of Earth!

130

Zetta was often in the cabin when I was brought in for my meal. Once, when Zetta and I were alone, I glanced behind us to see Brea's giant figure lurking in the doorway, watching us. I caught a glimpse of her face—white, thin-lipped, with eyes that seemed to smolder with fury.

"Zetta, is that Brea ever left near you? Alone with you?"

"I watch her then."

"She's there now in the passage doorway. Don't forget, she tried to have you murdered."

"She would not dare to harm me here—he would kill her. And," she added, "perhaps we may make use of her on Earth. You think of that?"

At other times, Graff was constantly questioning me. The chaos which Xenephrene's coming into this orbit had brought to Earth seemed intensely interesting to him. He seemed to have a keen knowledge of astronomy and we talked of the changed inclination of the Earth's axis, the changed climate. He questioned me about the different countries—most of them were only names to him—about the range of climate change, its intensity, its power of devastation to the crops and general welfare of the people in these various areas.

From Graff I learned that there were already on Earth several hundred of his men. They had with them only a small battery with which they could fling around them the crimson barrage in case of emergency.

I said, "That crimson barrage was all you had yourself when you were on earth before?"

"Yes. But now is different. I have other weapons. I have some ten thousand men. Over one thousand insects."

And there were several thousand women and children —the Braun race, Earth's future rulers, arriving in other vehicles, large and small. The vehicle we were on had the main equipment, the scientific apparatus for war. And I, aboard this vehicle, stood helpless.

Graff said, "Zetta tell me you might be able to draw me a map of Earth. Can you?"

"I can draw you one, fairly accurate, on the old Mercator's projection," I answered. "That is, the surface spread flat;

the lines of latitude and longitude at right angles rather than in a simulation of the globular surface."

He nodded. It took perhaps two hours. He never left my side, watching intently every stroke I made. When I had the main national bounderies sketched in, he stopped me.

"Show me where is the daylight now," he said.

I calculated. It was now, by Earth-time, the noon of July 7, 1971: almost exactly mid-spring in the north and mid-autumn in the south. The days and nights were now about equal at the equator—each some twelve hours long, shading off into twilight at the poles.

"And next month?" said Graff.

"The nights are lengthening in the south. The days are lengthening in the north." I went into this cycle more fully with him.

Then he said, "It is my plan to select a base. From there we can move within our barrage over any area of the country we wish—over air, land, sea. We can mount the barrage projectors on our platforms. They will fly; and they will float upon earth's water."

We discussed it for another hour. Midnight came; Zetta served us with food and hot drink. Graff spoke on and on, telling me smugly of his plans to destroy what he could of Earth until such time as the leading governments would acknowledge his supremacy.

Racing against his words were my thoughts of the impotence of my world against this kind of onslaught. First, even if available, our most powerful weapons could not be used: the annihilation, devastation to our own people, barred them automatically. Then, this infrared protection of the enemy. Could it be penetrated?

But Graff seemed tireless. He persisted with his outline of battle, with his questions.

He said, "Tell me what weapons they will use against me."

I explained in general the armaments of the nations: that it was all chaotic since the Great Change. Indeed, I was sure of very little I said! Most of the world capitals had moved. All the races and centers of population had shifted.

132

Nations were dissolving, disintegrating, blending as their people moved in wholesale flight to new areas.

In a few years the world would have been united almost like one big family, it would seem. There had been no thought, since the Great Change, of maintaining national armaments. The worst possible time to have an invader from another planet attack us! But this latter I did not explain to Graff.

At last I was free to go to my cabin. Graff remained with Zetta.

As I passed the closed doors on each side of me, a thought occurred to me. Why not take one desperate chance now? What had I to lose?

I looked about me. There was no one, nothing in sight. My heart was beating furiously. I crept to the first of the closed doors before me. With utmost caution, I tried turning its handle. Abruptly I wrenched free, my fingers trembling, tingling from the shock I had received.

So this was the answer! This was why Graff gave little heed to locking me in or having me guarded! Back in my cabin, with the door closed, I examined my shaking hand. No harm done. But the realization swept me: had I persisted in turning the handle, the chances were that I would have been electrocuted!

This tyrant was taking no chances with the safety of his treacherous weapons. And I remembered Zetta's warning: "Peter, do not take chances. You will gain nothing but possible death to yourself. Wait—until we are on Earth."

XVIII

THE EARTH AT BAY

HISTORY WILL record that the forces of Graff, the Xenephrene, landed upon Earth at 2 A.M. July 9, 1971, in north Brazil, at one degree, fourteen minutes north latitude, and

133

sixty-one degrees, twenty-two minutes west longitude. There was no one person on Earth who saw more than a fragment of what followed during those frightful weeks. Out of a myriad accounts, history will piece a pallid, dispassionate vision of the whole.

For myself, I witnessed many horrible things. But only fragments, as an ant with its tiny viewpoint sees the forest through which it crawls, and might futilely try to describe it. I can only name facts; imagination must supply the rest, and even then inevitably fall far short of the grim, tragic reality.

I was crouching with Graff and Zetta at a floor window of the giant space liner when, that July 9, we slowly settled to within a thousand feet of the ground. A dark, tropic, overcast night was outside.

From beneath our bow a crimson, howling radiance, one of the barrage projectors, sprang downward. There was no one left alive over the ten-mile circular area around which our barrage was flung that night, to tell what happened. I saw the houses of this newly-settled agricultural area melt and vanish as we swept them with our radiance.

The barrage went up. By dawn, all the country near us was deserted of its people, who fled in terror as far away from us as they could get.

The tropic jungle had wilted since the Great Change. The land here was cleared: broad, fertile fields, planted now with grain corn and garden produce. There were prosperous farms, crowded with settlers in their small, new houses; new villages; several small cities. Yet an area of over a hundred miles was deserted in a single day!

Graff's other vehicles arrived. One was dispatched to Africa, it landed in the Sudan, not far south of the city of Timbuktu, which had tripled in size and importance since the Great Change. The red barrage was flung up there, but it was on the flying platforms. Within a day it began moving directly north.

Round our encampment in north Brazil, the barrage projectors were mounted on the ground for a permanent stay. Its ten-mile circle included a stream; I found Graff had ap-

134

paratus for distilling the water, for drinking supply. He foraged out for food, even though he had a three months' supply with him. He began building houses for his women and children, using material he had brought and materials his insects dragged in from neighboring abandoned villages.

I was forced to stand by helplessly and watch this incredible activity. By the end of July his permanent base was well established. Earth had been attacked. I can only hint at the surprise and panic which Graff's landing caused all over the world. Since the Great Change, the last thing that had been given serious thought was the possibility of war.

The nations were concerned with their bare existence: the survival of their people. War between nations here was an impossiblity. The great battle forces of Britain, France, the United States and Russia were no longer armed for combat. Most all equipment had been dismantled of its armament, converted into reenforced transports for the people in distress and for the transportation of food and transplanting of people to a livable section of the globe.

I learned that armies had been organized as government and industrial and agricultural workers. Every government was in the business of producing, buying, selling, and storing food. The war planes were used exclusively for transportation to the more difficult areas. Thousands of the great modern Arctic A type were in commission, but few of them were armed at all.

The world was wholly unprepared and unequipped for war.

Nevertheless, Graff's base in north Brazil was attacked!

Railroad lines were near us. They were abandoned to traffic within fifty miles of us. But an armored train was run up wholly unexpectedly in the night and shelled us. One of Graff's foraging parties outside the barrage and therefore unprotected was struck and most of its members killed. But the screaming onslaught of shells which came all that night at twenty minute intervals exploded harmlessly against our invulnerable barrage.

The train with its thirty-mile range gun was gone at

135

dawn. But it came again the next night. I assumed it had not realized how little the damage was that it was capable of inflicting. Graff ordered me to accompany him and we went aloft on a small platform, high over our lines. Through the red glow of our barrage we could see the train in the distance—a blur of moving lights. Graff's platform carried a single small projector. At dawn, we sailed out through a momentary planned break in the barrage. The train saw us coming. It retreated, swinging and swaying at an eighty-mile-an-hour gait. It was a Garga trackless model, almost silent in its movements as it careened away from us.

But we caught it. Graff's face was exultant as he looked upon its ruins. There was nothing there the next instant but a tumbled heap of disfigured steel parts.

Graff gave the signal. The barrage opened briefly and we were back on the base.

A moment later, I realized the Garga onslaught was obviously used as a blind, a distraction—for suddenly there was a great roar in the skies. The Alaska jets, an armada of them, solid, spreading, streamed toward us in formation, one pilot slightly in the lead, heading straight for our camp. I wanted to shout to them. Perhaps I did—to warn them that no success could lie here for them with this protective barrage, only death to themselves.

I turned away so that I could not see the tragic end to their attack. They, their jets, turned into nothingness!

The world, during these swift-moving days, must have been frantically reassembling its armaments: those that could be brought into action without too much delay, and those which would not bring devastation or annihilation to the peoples of the Earth.

Graff's Brazil base continued to be harassed. By July 15, the river there quite suddenly went dry. Graff found through a scout that some fifty miles up the river on a distant rise of ground they had mounted a strangely-fashioned projector. It might have been from Xenephrene itself!

It was Freddie's heat projector! It had been sent here

136

from Miami by the United States government. We were to learn it had an effective range of some two miles, and its heat—they must have been applying it secretively, continuously for several days—had dried up the small watercourse, sending it up in clouds of steam!

Graff ordered an attacking platform out. It never returned, was never heard from again. Then we found that, still farther up, they were damming our stream. Graff left them alone. He sent foraging parties at intervals for water. They were frequently attacked.

From Zetta, I sometimes had accounts of these hand-to-hand engagements. Graff had a variety of small hand weapons with which his foraging men were armed: hand batteries of the purple Reet-current. They shot very short purple stabs of flame. I recalled seeing the guards use them that night at the Garla Stadium.

There were hand knives, not unlike the Spanish machete. And occasionally Graff used a lethal gas which clung its weight close to the ground. The wind would sometimes sweep it over a village.

The small purple flame projectors interested me particularly, and I persuaded Graff to show me one. The crimson barrage was a form of Reet; so was this purple light. The one had a low vibration rate, the other a high one. Both, of course, were akin to the Control globes. I tried again to mention the Control with the sweeping devastation it held harnessed. But Graff shut me up. He was not using it yet. I found out soon afterward that by every artifice in her power, Zetta was holding him back.

But he explained the purple flame. It stabbed into the crimson barrage, neutralized it. With one of these small projectors, a man at a distance of ten feet could stab a small hole through our red radiance. Graff had his men use this small hand projector to blind the earthmen at short range, and to explode their weapons in their hands.

I said casually, "The Garlands had these purple projectors?"

"Of course, Peter."

137

"Graff, why couldn't that be made in a larger form? A giant purple beam?"

"It could. The Garlands have it."

My thoughts were running tumultuously. Father, Dan and Freddie were up there in Garla. I said, still casually, "Then the Garlands could have penetrated our barrage—neutralized it?"

He smiled lugubriously. "Yes," he said.

Graff was in a good mood this day. He showed me some of the defensive apparatus he had brought along: insulated garments which one might wear and be protected, at least partially, from the red barrage; infrared goggles to protect the sight; ear grids to bar out the sound, to raise it again to the normal vibration to which our human ears are accustomed.

"Why," I said, "with these one might walk through our barrage!"

"Yes," he agreed. "I should not care to try it, but one might get through safely."

He put them away.

We had no reports from Africa. But later I learned it was over there that, in these early days, the greatest damage to Earth was done. The flying ring of platforms, ordered there by Graff, with the vehicle in their midst, had immediately begun moving northward.

Slowly but inexorably, some two or three hundred miles a day, impervious to every attack that could be sent against them, they blazed a ten-mile twisting trail northward across Africa—a trail of blank, dead-gray surface of empty earth.

It was as though some giant finger of death were dragging itself over the continent. It cut a swath through Timbuktu, trailed over the newly settled, newly fertile Sahara, swung east over the mountains into the erstwhile Libyan desert. Then north over the Mediterranean. It was there by July 20.

A fleet of warships, hastily assembled from every nation, was in the Mediterranean. The red enemy flew high. Its barrage was downward. The ships, at a fair distance, withstood the red glow. Especially at night. The crimson screaming radiance appeared to be more deadly then, but it was not. Our sunlight was favorable to it; by day its range and power were greatly increased.

I warned Graff not to destroy these ships: I told him he would have use for them at a later date himself. Zetta agreed and told him to heed my advice.

He nodded his approval. But one ship, south of Malta, was caught in a fringe of outflung red beam. Those on board have told me what for a minute or two they went through. It was night. The ship's lights went out: its dynamos were burned. There were several explosions aboard. But the ship escaped. Its men were half deafened, their eyes were red, smarting and strained, and they suffered a weird irritation of the skin. Many were laughing with an hysteria which no one could explain.

The last week in July saw Graff spreading out in South America. His permanent camp housed the women, children and older men. They maintained the barrage. The insects were working with the men building the town.

With a ring of flying platforms, Graff made a sortie north. He had further business there. At his command, I had prepared a small metal cylinder and written his dictated message:

"*To the governments of the Earth, from Graff, the Xenephrene.*"

There is no need to repeat here the grandiose language and threats included. He boasted that the people of the Earth would, if they valued their lives, soon swear allegiance to his government, to him. He gave them the choice of complete and absolute surrender or complete annihilation. He directed the Miami authorities that when this message was received, they should notify us by a swaying white searchlight beam from Miami Beach the following night. Graff would wait two nights after that; then, the night of August 7, if the beam showed again swaying, he would know they desired to yield. But if it stood straight up into the sky, motionless, he would understand they still defied him.

The cylinder was dropped into the outskirts of Miami.

139

It went down, flaming like a beacon from the blazing gas we had ignited in its top.

After some hours, a giant searchlight was erected at Miami Beach. It swayed its answer that the cylinder had been found and Graff's message was being considered.

We hung fifty miles high, waiting.

I have been told, and I can fairly imagine, the scene at the conference which was held in the Miami War Department during those three following long days with the brief nights in between them.

At this daylight season there was a freight and passenger air line flying from Miami to the Canaries for the recently established capitals of Great Britain and France near the Barbary Coast.

Upon one of these liners representatives of all the European governments came hastily to assemble at Miami. From Japan came leaders of the Oriental powers; and from Caracas, the greatest capital now of South America, came the newly elected President of the Pan American Union. The world powers held a grave, solemn conference that August 6. I understand it lasted without intermission for some thirty-six hours.

They decided to yield.

The conference ended on the night of August 7. From the War Department a telephone was connected with the little house at the beach where the operator was ready to flash the signal. Our War Secretary rose to his feet.

"Shall I give the word now, gentlemen?" They say his voice nearly broke.

There was a silent assent.

From the adjoining room a telephone rang sharply—then another. There was confusion in there: telephones ringing, and the government radio sounding a peremptory incoming call. Confusion, while the War Secretary stood irresolute. Then an Under Secretary burst into the room. He shouted,

"A globe from space has landed in the Everglades!"

A few moments, and from a dozen sources came the de-

140

tails. Professor Vanderstuyft had arrived from Xenephrene! With him were his daughter, Daniel Cain, Frederick Smith —and a young man named Kean, a Xenephrene friendly to Earth. They had weapons with them which were to fight this invader!

They were no more than fifty miles from Miami, and were being rushed to the conference by a government Arctic A.

We were crouching over the floor of our hovering globe, gazing down at the shadowy outlines of the Florida coast. The twilight of August 7 deepened into night. No searchlight showed.

We did not see father's vehicle come down; I knew nothing about it until afterward.

The hours passed. "They will yield," said Graff confidently. "They postpone now the humiliating hour. But before the dawn we shall see their searchlight beam."

And Zetta and I thought so too. The short night passed; the faint light of dawn began showing. And then the white beam from down there sprang up.

It stood vertical! Motionless!

For a moment we stared at it, unbelieving. Moisture clouded my sight of it. My brave world, firmly shining its defiance!

Graff sprang to his feet. "Incredible! They have not yielded?"

Anger contorted his face; chagrin was in his voice. I think he felt the rebuff more strongly for Zetta's presence.

"So they will not yield? The worse for them! You shall see now the Red Control, Peter!"

XIX

RED MADNESS STALKING THE EARTH

Days of grim activity in Graff's camp followed. Near the north line of our barrage Graff built a small stone house.

141

Within it the control globes were being erected. Above our camp a flying platform constantly hovered. It spread a thin red barrage of protection above us.

On the afternoon of August 14 current was turned into the globes. They hummed gently. When the twilight and night came, I saw them emitting a faint purple radiance. Within an hour it hung over all the inside area of the camp like a purple haze—the haze I had seen in the air of Xenephrene. It was to protect us here, in our enclosed area, from the effects of this thing we were about to broadcast over the Earth!

A week from that night when Graff had been defied by Earth, he was ready. It had been a terrifying, anxious week for me. A thousand times I had thought of vague plans of something desperate to do. But what? I was closely guarded every minute now. Even Zetta appeared to have someone at her side at all times.

During the evening of August 14, while I was watching the purple haze, Graff sought me. Zetta was with him.

"We are ready, Peter. You and Zetta will want to see these small globes that are so powerful to triumph for us. I am going now to turn on the current into the Red Globe."

We walked over the slightly undulating dead-gray waste of what had been the Brazilian farm country. We had returned to our base there. The ground was covered with a gray dust, like burned powder.

The stone house was set close behind the barrage, bathed in its crimson light—a small one-storied house with no windows. The room we entered was tiny, with one small white light. My personal guards had been ordered to wait outside. The two interior guards wore goggles and eargrids, tight trousers and smocks of black insulating fabric, caps with black masks now raised—and black gloves.

The room had one interior doorway, a small round opening with a heavy bullseye door. We stooped to pass through, emerging into a low, black-vaulted room. On a small railed platform stood the two small globes. Another man was here, robed in the black tight-fitting garments—gloved, masked and goggled. Grotesque executioner!

142

There was a tense moment. The room was dim and dead silent. The two globes were white, opaque and silent. Graff turned to a switch.

For the first time that evening Zetta spoke, an involuntary cry of protest. "No! Graff—no!"

She gripped him but he thrust her roughly aside. I was tense. I think then I was about to leap upon Graff in a suicidal attempt to protect Zetta and stop this man from what he was about to commit. But from the hand of the black-robed man a weapon was pointing quietly and menacingly at me.

Zetta gasped, "No, Peter! Do nothing—"

Throughout all this, Graff's face was grimly inscrutable. He reached up abruptly and threw the switch; the dim light from somewhere in the room faded and vanished. A crimson glow from one of the globes took its place. The other globe stood milk-white, silent, ready.

A humming. From the grid over the active globe a faint red beam was streaming. It spread, deepened, streamed out through the solid black wall of the room. I stared after it—sidewise, upward. I seemed too be gazing out into a black, illimitable distance, red-tinted. Long, unearthly vibrations, broadcast now around the world! They were already around and back again and starting anew.

"Come!" said Graff. "We must make haste—get out of here—"

The black-masked operator was seated at his small table, watching his dials. The red globe had settled to its steady hum when we left the room. It had been a strangely brief scene—yet I have never witnessed a scene of such horror. A small stone house, a black-vaulted room with its lone, black-garbed man. One small globe, faintly humming, glowing crimson.

But I knew that within days our great Earth would be at its mercy!

Back on Xenephrene in Garla, that evening at the Stadium, there had followed a night of confusion. With the infrared Control stolen, the Garlands were in a panic. The frightened

143

people had rushed for the grottos. By the time the authorities were able to bring order, the night had passed. At dawn, pursuit had started for the Braun city. But it was too late—Graff's expedition had left for Earth. The Brauns remaining on Xenephrene, as well as the people of Garla, learned now, too late, of Graff's duplicity! Without the infrared Control, they were all doomed within a few months.

The only available vehicle for father, Dan, Freddie, Hulda and Kean was the one in which I had gone to Xenephrene from Earth. It took almost a week for them to gather weapons and equipment with which to fight Graff. If on Earth the Control was recovered, Kean would race back with it to Garla.

It was a long journey for father's party. They dropped into the Everglades August 7. Father, reaching the Conference, argued against surrender, and the delegates from the world powers, heartened by the weapons from Xenephrene, reversed their decision.

There was much to do before Graff could be seriously attacked. Four Arctic A jets had to be equipped with the four purple ray projectors. There was also the crimson barrage projector to be assembled and mounted—and a fighting force of some two hundred jets, whose pilots and gunners were all to wear the insulated black garb from Xenephrene.

Freddie and Dan, chafing at their enforced inactivity, persuaded the authorities to let them try Freddie's heat ray in advance of the main Earth attack. His projector could create, within a two-mile range, a heat of some three hundred degrees Fahrenheit. It had a three-mile range if the heat was concentrated to a six-foot striking area. Graff's barrage was vertical; its horizontal area of danger was no more than five hundred feet.

In a muffled, unlighted plane, selecting a dark night, Freddie and Dan might with luck get within a few miles of the barrage. There was no one who could say whether the heat vibrations of Freddie's projector might or might not penetrate the crimson glow.

They planned to start on the night of August 15. By the evening of August 14 they were in the Miami War Depart-

144

ment, receiving last instructions. The official radio was droning its routine messages.

There was a sudden interference—a chaos of weird voices! The interference grew worse; then the radio went dead. The telegraphs, telephones and undersea cables all had sudden interference, but they kept in operation. The new "invisible light-beam" phones, as they were popularly called, maintained service under difficulty. The electric lights went dim, almost out.

All this happened within a few minutes, that evening of August 14. In Miami and all over the world, it was the same. And then, almost unnoticed at first, slowly inexorably the reign of the Red Madness began.

It began with a feeling of uneasiness, an oppression: the feeling one sometimes has when the barometer falls in the lull before a coming storm. The countries in the daylight felt it most strongly.

The sick, the weak, the nervous were the most quickly effected. In hospitals there was a sudden hysteria among the patients. An elderly woman patient ran, laughing and screaming that red demons were after her. She was, perhaps, the first of millions.

She leaped into the street. Freddie and Dan recall her shuddering scream and eerie laughter as it floated into the open windows of the War Department there in Miami.

And at the War Department itself the reports from abroad were increasingly alarming. Within an hour every official channel, set up in frantic haste, was cluttered with news. From every quarter of the Earth medical authorities, scientific bodies and conglomeration of government officials were demanding an explanation from Miami.

And then the world of the infrared began showing. Vague red shapes were in the air, muttering, chattering.

The confusion of the Miami authorities was intensified by the red hysteria, adding to the handicap of weather conditions. Hulda was there; she says it was a bedlam.

Father, Freddie and Dan were busy getting the equipment they had brought from Xenephrene into hasty use.

Then Freddie and Dan had the heat projector hastily

transferred to a Nungess monoplane-type flyer—a tiny affair, soundless, best for their purpose. They donned suits of the black insulated fabric; they had the glasses and ear-grids, and beside the heat-projector a small Essen-Bloc airplane gun.

Within two hours they left the chaos of the War Department, took off from an adjacent stage for Graff's Brazilian encampment. They left with the assurance that the Earth's main attack would follow them in a few days. A few days! If the workmen assembling the weapons could hold their reason. The War Secretary laughed a little wildly as he said it. White-faced Hulda flung her arms around Dan and wept. She could not believe that she would ever see him again.

XX

THE NIGHT PROWLERS

"WHERE THE DEVIL are we?" demanded Dan. "These instruments are useless! And I can't see anything—"

They had run into a gale from the north, soon after crossing over Cuba. Flying with it, they had made great speed over Jamaica, across the Caribbean, to strike the Colombian coast near the mouth of the river below Baranquilla.

They swept southward. Dan was anxiously, fearfully watching for the dawn. The red things were riding the night with the plane; they seemed to crowd the cabin, their voices jabbering over the muffled motor-throb.

Then faintly, far ahead through the overcast night, the crimson glow of Graff's barrage was streaming above the horizon.

Dan swung them down as Freddie lifted his glasses and eyed the landscape through his minature telescope. They had to determine the location of the Red Control, and then rush it.

"Off, Dan. Close enough!"

"Too close!" Dan muttered. "If they spot us—"

It would be complete failure. Every moment Dan and Freddie feared the Control would tilt down with its beam darting at them. They could withstand it but their plane could not.

"Freddie! What's that?"

On the dead-gray surface of the ground ahead of them, two black blobs showed: black-garbed figures running away from the barrage. One blob leaped ahead, then waited. The other was running steadily—heavily—

From the Control house—after that brief scene when Graff turned the current into the crimson globe—Zetta and I were led back to the encampment. Graff gave orders to my guard, and left us, busy with his other duties. The guard seemed to be out of earshot, so I whispered to Zetta:

"I must do something tonight, something to stop that damned thing—"

"Hush, Peter. He will hear you. Go to bed—please. Trust me. I know best."

She leaped away before I could answer, leaving me standing there.

I occupied a lone little house. My room had one barred door and two barred windows. My guard sat by the door.

I went to bed but could not sleep. The darkness of my room seemed luminous with purple haze—the protecting purple glow which hung about the camp. The world outside had no such protection. The broadcast crimson vibrations were seeking out every tiny corner of the Earth.

I must have drifted off. I was awakened by a hand over my mouth. A dark form was beside me in the blackness. A voice murmured in my ear:

"Peter. Don't struggle!"

Zetta's voice! I relaxed. Then I sat up. I could see her dimly. She was dressed in a tight-fitting black smock, with tight long trousers to her ankles, joining black cloth shoes. There was a black hood, pushed back with dangling mask

147

and black gloves pulled up over her tight black sleeves. Complete insulation!

"Here, Peter—put these on. Hurry!"

She thrust garments at me. Then a long curved pod-knife. "Use it if you have to. I will lead. Hurry—"

I sensed her shudder. The knife was wet; I knew why. In the darkness outside, my guard lay motionless, sprawled face down on the ground. Zetta leaped. I stepped over him. She waited for me, then leaped lightly forward again.

The camp was dark and silent; we avoided a low-humming purple projector. I ran, with Zetta leaping ahead of me. We got safely past the houses. The insects were quartered at the opposite end of town. None were allowed abroad at night; I was thankful for that.

The night was overcast—darker, it seemed, than before. I wondered how near dawn it was. Probably very near. Zetta came to the bed of the dry watercourse, jumped down into it. I climbed down, thirty feet perhaps. In the blackness I ran forward.

Zetta was now at my side, clutching one of my hands, trying to draw me on. A guard from the bank appeared suddenly over our heads. He called sharply. Zetta answered. She leaped up and stood beside him, speaking to him to hold his attention. I crept up through the gloom, and lunged with the knife. He fell.

The barrage line at last was before us. Its red glow bathed the bottom of the river bed. Zetta stopped me.

"You get your breath, Peter. Then, we race. We will be through it in a few minutes."

We were adjusting our glasses, strapping on the ear-grids.

"Zetta, where did you get these?"

"From Brea!" The red illumination showed her faint, ironical smile. "She and I, we have been planning it for a long time. She wants that I never see Graff again; and so she help us escape. I did not tell her we would try for the Control house!"

"And me? Why help me escape?"

"I tol' her that if we escape, we would marry. You see?

148

Then I would be lost to Graff forever. So she steal these equipment—"

My arms went around her. It was a strange time for lovemaking, but my emotions overcame me. "Marry, Zetta? Then, you do love me?"

She pushed me away. "Come. There is no time for that now—"

At the edge of the narrow barrage a guard was standing on the river bank. He flung a tiny white beam down on us. Zetta called to him, tried to lure him down.

But abruptly he shouted an alarm. From across the river another figure came in a leap, sailing over our heads. We ducked into a hole. Above us the two guards stood consulting.

No general alarm seemed to have been given; these two guards doubtless were the only ones at this section.

"Zetta, call again! Distract them—I'll climb up."

I could hear Zetta calling up something about Graff. I climbed up behind them. I lunged. One stabbed at me with a short purple flame—but it missed, or my insulated garments killed it. As they stood together, I struck with my knife and flailing arms. I could feel their flimsy bodies crack. They sank at my feet.

We started away, running. We went through the barrage. With the glasses on, the barrage was all the dead gray of night. And soundless. But I could feel it plucking at me. Once I got the impression I was almost wading through it, fighting it. A fear that was almost panic seized me. I laughed, to ward it off. I was laughing when Zetta gripped me, jerked off the glasses and my mask.

"Peter! Stop that! You are all right!"

The night air steadied me. We were in the darkness, well beyond the barrage. It was perhaps a mile to the Control house. We followed the barrage line, creeping, running, taking advantage of every gully. Garbed in black, we were doubtless not easy to see. There was no alarm given.

The dawn was near. A guard near the Control house came up to us. Fortunately he had not seen from which direction we had come. He was less suspicious than the

149

others: our outfits were more to be expected here near
the Control. Zetta told him we were from Graff. He sank
soundlessly as my knife slashed his throat.

The two guards in the outer room were almost equally
easy. But one let out a shout. The Control-keeper came out at
us. My fist crushed his face.

We were in the Control room! The crimson globe stood
there murmuring. Diabolical thing! With my gloved hands,
I ripped at it—tore its wires, tumbled it down, kicked and
wrecked it with a passionate frenzy.

"Enough, Peter. Help me with this."

Zetta had been swiftly unfastening the inert purple
globe. She gathered up its mechanism, handed it all to me.

"Here—be careful—"

It weighed only a few pounds. It seemed not unduly
fragile and I put it under my arm. We were outside again
in a couple of minutes. No one accosted us this time. Graff
may have been a genius, but he was inexperienced in war
and sabotage. There were no other guards about.

Again we ran—north, over the gray empty country,
striving to escape being seen. But what a distance lay before
us! I figured that heading northeast was best, but it might
be a hundred miles or more before we encountered anyone.
The wrecked Control would be discovered by Graff, and
pursuit would follow. Perhaps I had better send Zetta on
ahead with this purple globe. Send her on to safety.

To one side of us, in the darkness, a shape suddenly took
form. A small plane, flying low. An Earth airplane! This
could be no enemy! Zetta had been leaping ahead of
me, waiting after each leap as I plowed along. We stood
together, and I waved my arms.

A small white searchlight caught us as the plane passed
close overhead. I flung back my hood and mask to meet the
light. The plane circled, came back, landed on the level
gray expanse.

In a moment we were with the amazed Dan and Freddie,
and the precious purple globe was on board. The twilight
of dawn was silvering our plane as we headed northwest,
flying for Miami.

XXI

A NEST OF VERMIN

THERE ARE SOME things that may be pictured by a shuddering imagination. But one does not voluntarily put them
into spoken words. History will say only that for twenty-
four hours, August 14 and 15 of 1971, our Earth was swept
by a wild insanity.

The burning of Cape Town by a mob gone mad will
be mentioned—the glare of the city against the night sky;
the thousands who, bereft of reason, cast themselves with
screams into the flames. The wrecking of two great surface
liners, with three thousand lives lost, and the major riots
in a dozen cities will be described. But history will only
hint at the highlights—it cannot tell of all the million
individual incidents. Crazed men and women attacked the
Biskra arsenal, and the frenzied, crazed soldiers waded
heedlessly into the mob, firing wildly. Then there were the
ten government planes circling over the city whose pilots,
crazed by the red madness and what they saw in the
streets, fired down with machine guns and then plunged
into the crowd. Lone criminals, crazed by the madness that
took everyone, prowled the dark streets in search of victims.

It is best that the Red Madness be forgotten.

It was late in the afternoon of August 15 before the
frantic chemists could reassemble the purple globe and begin the broadcasting of its healing waves. All that evening
they were flung out around the world. The Red Madness, in
a few hours, would be gone.

By midnight, the "etherplane," as scientists now term it,
had regained normality. The current was cut from the
purple globe. The world rested, exhausted, bewildered,
gazing back stupefied at what it had been through.

For hours more, governments, soldiers and police, with

151

sanity regained at last, fought wearily with the eddies and backwash of the storm. It wore itself out, and order was restored. There remained the smoking ruins of property destroyed, and the dead, the maimed, and the thousands of poor miserable creatures with reason permanently gone.

A single day of the Red Madness! May there never be, on this or any other world, another day such as that!

Kean was to take back the purple globe to Xenephrene. We all stood in the Miami War Department, prepared to see him off.

He said, "My worl' has brought great disaster upon you. But I think you will defeat Graff easily now."

Our unified forces had gathered in groups; our air force was in readiness, without fear now of being swallowed in the Red Control. We were all tense with the thought of the coming battle.

Kean said, "Now, as I leave, you will not mind that I tell you I love Hulda? You know it. But I would say it and wish you, Dan, much happiness with her." He was twinkling but his voice was solemn.

He bowed quaintly; his fingers barely touched Hulda's outstretched hand. He left us hastily.

From the roof of the War Department we watched his tiny globe ascending into the star-filled night. Would he reach Xenephrene safely? Father thought so. And he told us then what astronomers, just before the Red Madness, had discovered. Xenephrene had broken the orbit of her eclipse around the sun! She seemed to be heading outward again, leaving our solar system. Father said that he also believed that with the departure of Xenephrene, our Earth's axis might swing back to its former inclination.

On the morning of August 18, our air force was ready to start. From Brazil news came that it was thought that Graff was planning a new flight of devastation with his flying platforms. But it never took place: our attack was first.

Our expedition consisted of a hundred and fifty Arctic

152

A warplanes, each with three men, pilot and gunners. We were all garbed in the black garments with glasses and ear-grids. One plane carried nothing but our lone crimson ray. Four other planes carried the four purple-ray projectors and Essen-Bloc long range guns. The rest carried only the Essen-Blocs and the short-range, old-fashioned machine gun.

Dan, Freddie and I were to fly together. Our plane carried a purple projector, an Essen-Bloc, and a machine gun. We were chosen to lead the expedition because of our familiarity with the Garland weapons and my knowledge of Graff's lines.

The most skillful, the most daring young pilots of the world—the pick of a dozen nations—comprised the force we commanded. The plane carrying the crimson projector was flown by Davis and Robertson, sons of the men who had given their lives attacking the Xenephrenes near New York during Graff's first invasion.

We were all linked together by the modern Rand system of air phones—the first time it had been given a full and practical demonstration. For a hurried test we circled that morning above Miami. Dan ordered the expedition to wheel, to loop, to execute a variety of movements in concert to prove its ability, with so brief a time for coordination, to maintain the skilled precision so imperative to our attack.

The people thronged Miami's streets, roof-tops and terraces and cheered and cried out, wishing us well. Biscayne Bay was crowded with boats, perilously loaded with cheering mobs.

I had just a moment alone with Zetta before we started. How many warriors, in all the ages, of every race and every time, have parted thus upon the eve of battle from the woman they loved!

"Zetta—you too are sure, aren't you?" I said softly. She came suddenly into my arms, her lips seeking mine. She whispered, "Yes, Peter. I am sure!"

All my dreams of all my life came into reality with the coming of her love.

153

In the sunlight of that morning of August 18, our shining planes left the Lauderdale airport and roared southward.

It was full night when, out of the star-lit sky, we sighted Graff's barrage. Our four planes with the purple ray were leading; the others were massed below and behind us. Graff had a brief warning, no doubt. We were several miles off when one of his red beams swung down. We could see it coming—a broad band of crimson, like a giant searchlight beam.

It missed us with its first swing. Dan roared his orders into the Rand-phone. I was at the controls. I headed the ship down, in advance of our line, to protect the planes behind us. Freddie leveled our projector. Its narrow purple beam sprang forward at the barrage. Behind us the planes were strung out. Davis and Robertson were well behind, for safety precaution. And we were determined not to use the crimson projector in the mélée of battle. It would confuse our other vehicles and be too dangerous to them. We also wanted to protect it in case of a last, desperate need. Davis and Robertson were ordered to keep close behind our purple rays.

This showing of our purple ray was Graff's first knowledge that here on Earth the Garland weapons were to be used against him. There must have been panic sweeping the Xenephrene camp at that instant!

Freddie evidently had caught the range. Our purple light mingled with the crimson—mingled and merged into a vacant blackness through which the farther stars showed dimly. The whole front crescent of the barrage swung down at us now; but our four purple beams held it.

We roared forward. Black holes of neutral emptiness were ahead. The front face of the Xenephrene red line was broken by our rays.

At two miles we began firing the Essen-Blocs. Graff's crimson beams were wavering confusion now from every part of the line. Some of our shells were caught and fired in mid-air, but many got through. It was soon a chaos, as we darted in. It was to be one brief, desperate, reckless at-

154

tack. There was not a man of us who had been willing to plan it otherwise.

At a mile, we could no longer hold our communication. The air was snapping and hissing with its mingling, warring vibrations. The phones went dead. Each plane now had to act for itself.

I headed ours straight in. Freddie was firing the Essen at swift intervals. Our purple light held steady before us, boring its black hole in the confusion of crimson—a black hole into which Freddie was firing as I headed our plane into it.

Only a few minutes passed, but they seemed like hours. We were so close now that beams from the side angles of the barrage were coming at us, missing by inches.

I had taken off my glasses and ear-grids for a moment. The night was a confusion of hissing, crossing beams. Vivid glares—crimson and purple, merging black. A myriad sparks snapping around us—and ahead, a growing yellow-red glare of distant buildings burning. Our shells were finding their mark!

A chaos of bursting color and sound!

Dan growled at me, "Look over us, Peter. Damn that fellow Davis—look where he's going!"

Our other three planes, carrying the purple projectors, were flying level with me. But most of the others had climbed.

The barrage beams were all swinging out and downward. I could see a hundred of our planes in a group mounting to climb over the camp. Davis and Robertson were up there. The crimson beam of their projector showed for a moment, then went out. They seemed to be climbing higher than all the other planes—spiraling now, straight up. I lost sight of them.

A stray red beam caught some of the soaring planes. They came wavering down, spirals of light . . . vanishing. One melted as it passed near us—flickered into nothingness like a flame dying.

Our planes up there were firing downward. And then,

155

coming over Graff's line, they were dropping bombs. The yellow glare from the camp village was spreading.

We were now well over Graff's lines. Every one of our jets, save those which we had lost, was over the line now. The very desperation of our attack was irresistible; Graff had no time to prepare a defense. Once we were within his lines, his immobile ground defenses, his projectors, were impotent to harm us. The barrage was flickering, sections of it dark now even when our purple rays were turned aside. It was broken, flickering out.

Suddenly the whole barrage vanished completely, as one of our shells must have hit its power house.

Five hundred feet above the dead gray ground we flew in toward the camp itself. The barrage was gone; one single last beam came up from the river and as suddenly vanished.

Below us now the ground within Graff's lines was glaring yellow-red from the conflagation of the village. We could see the figures of people and the giant insects running in aimless panic. Our planes shot them down.

Flying platforms were standing in a long line, where Graff had had them ready for his new attack. Panic-stricken Brauns were crowding onto them. And from everywhere the flying platforms were trying to escape. Our planes attacked them. And far overhead I could now see Davis and Robinson's crimson beam. They were up there; and any vehicles which got past us they caught and annihilated.

From the river bank Graff's huge cylindrical space-liner now struggled up. Its end was gone. Smoke and flame were rising from its interior fittings. It rose laboriously, painted red-yellow with the lurid glare from below. I have often wondered if Graff was on it!

It evidently had no usable weapons. It rose heavily, with our jets darting after it like wasps, circling it, stabbing its huge vitals with shellfire. It did not get very high. It came down presently, turned completely over, crashed and broke into leaping flames and black smoke rolling up in a cloud.

I had guided our plane across the encampment and back,

156

then circled, as a score of our planes were circling. There were scenes down there in the burning town—where half an hour before more than fifteen thousand people had been living—scenes which now I do not like to remember. But it was a nest of vermin and we had to stamp it out.

Suddenly Davis and Robinson's plane appeared below us. Its red beam sprang downward! Under its crimson light the ground was turning blank! The burning village, the wrecked and burning vehicles, the panic-stricken people still alive, the dead bodies now strewn about—all melting, vanishing into nothingness.

Then we climbed and for a long time I did not look down again. When I did, the yellow-red glare of the conflagration had vanished. A circular ten-mile spread of blank, dead-gray ground lay beneath us. Over it some of our planes were circling low with white searchlights examining it.

There was absolutely nothing left.

XXII

PEACE ON EARTH

THERE WAS A year of adjustment; time for meditation. And many of us feel that, out of the tragedy and horror of those awful months, has come a benefit to our Earth. The Great Change brought all the nations, all the peoples of every race into a keen realization of values, an enforced community of interest. Like brothers in a family sorely pressed, they fought united against a ruthless, wrathful nature. Then came the invaders from Xenephrene.

Earth's supreme effort had been put forth: a united urge as we four hundred young men, representing all the world's nations, flew against Graff that night in Brazil. I think then we raised a monument to a new Earthly spirit. Our united

157

life, or death! That spirit of oneness will not easily be forgotten.

I sit here tonight, finishing these pages. A great thankfulness is upon me. Out of the horror of the past, I have come to this hour with a dear father still holding his strength and health. I have a beautiful, adoring wife, to realize every dream of my boyhood, to mother our lusty little son. I have a sister happily married to a man I respect. I have a bachelor friend, joyous with his lot!

This Earth has become a good place on which to live.

www.ingramcontent.com/pod-product-compliance
Lightning Source LLC
Chambersburg PA
CBHW032204190626

46810CB00018B/1551